Ambush Town...

Longarm rode into Placer Town late that night. He reckoned that Matt Forman was at least an hour ahead of him; but as he clopped down the main street, he saw no sign of the man, or of anyone else for that matter. The only light came from the window in the doc's office, but the saloons were dark, despite the horses lined up at the hitch racks in front of them, and the light on the hotel porch was out. Placer Town—and Matt Forman—was waiting for him.

Longarm took out his Colt, rested it on his thigh, and kept on riding, a lightning rod waiting for the first quick flash. It came, as he expected, without warning...

➤ TABOR EVANS ◄

LONGARM

IN THE
BIG BURNOUT

J

JOVE BOOKS, NEW YORK

LONGARM IN THE BIG BURNOUT

A Jove Book/published by arrangement with
the author

PRINTING HISTORY
Jove edition/May 1988

ISBN: 0-515-09548-6

Jove books are published by The Berkley Publishing Group,
200 Madison Avenue, New York, New York 10016.
The name "JOVE" and the "J" logo
are trademarks belonging to Jove Publications, Inc.

PRINTED IN THE UNITED STATES OF AMERICA

10 9 8 7 6 5 4 3 2 1

Chapter 1

The afternoon was half gone and the heat had reached a cruel intensity as Longarm rode east. Nothing relieved it. A hundred out here, he figured, maybe hotter—enough to curl a lizard's hide. The edges of his saddle were too hot for comfort and the metal pieces of the bridle sent painful glints into his eyes. He raised his bandanna over his nose to keep the stinging dust out of his nostrils.

It was near five before he lifted from the baked flat into rolling sand dunes and clay gulches. An occasional pine stood as lonely sentinel against the distant hills hanging before him, black and bulky and lofty, the narrow white streak of a road coiling upward to vanish in the timber. He crossed a shallow creek, pausing long enough to let his horse satisfy its thirst, then kept on until he reached the road and began his climb into the cool, shadowed bench lands.

A hundred feet or so above the desert floor, he turned and craned his neck to gaze back the way he had come. Yes, the rider was still in sight, as hard to catch with the eye as a flea on an old dog. Whether the rider was following Longarm or not was open to question. This was, after all, the only road through these hills, and Longarm did not have to be the only one with business in this part of the world.

Still, he considered it wise to keep an eye on the rider, just in case.

Turning back around, he urged his horse on across the long flat toward the distant foothills, eager to reach their cool, green ranks. As the sun sank at his back, his shadow stretched out farther and farther before him. Reaching the foothills at last, he turned to see if he could catch another glimpse of the man behind him. But the rider had vanished, swallowed up by the vast, prowling shadows growing now along the desert floor.

Lifting his head slightly, Longarm squinted into the red light, catching the last great burst of flame as the sun edged below the earth's rim. Instantly, the world was transformed into another place, blue and still, the air redolent with the smell of the pine-clad hills about him. A sweet coolness, coming from the distant peaks, flowed against him, taking some of the curse off the day's relentless heat. Turning around, he kept on into the foothills, following the rutted road that led between the sloping, timber-choked slopes.

He came to Placer Town well past dusk. It sat upon a bench facing the foothills, a double row of buildings on

2

either side of the main road, narrow streets branching off it, and more buildings scattered about in the semi-darkness on bare, timbered-off hills, or perched atop wooded gullies. Beyond the town, the road kept on into a canyon until it vanished into the sheer, vertical land of towering peaks that reared into the night sky above the town like shadowed, titanic guardians.

He let the road carry him across a booming, wooden-plank bridge and down the main street, past single-story houses, their lights blooming through dusty windows, casting a fitful light over the roadway ahead of him. At the center of town another road cut out of the hills to form an intersection. On the four corners sat a hotel, a store, and two saloons facing each other diagonally. One seemed to have no name, the other one was called The Owl Hoot, its sign freshly painted. Next to the other saloon was a livery stable, into which he rode.

An old man materialized out of the stable's gloom, looked closely at him, and said, "Third stall back."

Longarm gave his horse a small drink at the street trough before leading him into the livery, where he removed the horse's saddle and other gear, dropping the saddle over the partition separating the stalls. He stood for a moment in the stall, his big hand resting on the sweat-gummed back of the horse, then walked out into the street. Pausing, he lit his first cheroot of the day. The smoke had no flavor in his parched mouth, and he bent over the drinking trough's feed pipe and let the icy water roll into his throat and fill up his belly until it would hold no more. Straightening, he wiped off his mouth with the back of his hand and took a few satisfying puffs on his cheroot, then headed on into the smaller

3

saloon, his saddlebags slung over one shoulder, his war bag over the other.

It was the supper hour and slack time. He stood at the bar with no company except the barkeep, took his Maryland rye neat, and returned to the street, pausing on the porch to suck the cheroot's smoke into his lungs. He looked over this small, grim town huddled under the peaks' shadows, aware of a current of cool air flowing out of the mountains. The odor of food from the hotel across the street had an effect on him so immediate that a sharp pain started in the corners of his jaws. Men crossing the street moved idly in and out of the hotel, bound to and from supper. Others strolled past the saloon on the wooden walks, each one as he passed giving Longarm a quick, bold glance, making no effort to hide their curiosity. He was a stranger and they all knew it.

Across the street three men came out of The Owl Hoot and moved in a quiet group toward the hotel. As they entered it, another man left the hotel and started across the street toward Longarm, his tall, lanky form alternately clear, then dark, as he passed through the lamp-lit beams shining from nearby windows. There was a lean, sharp edge to his shoulders and a hard-brimmed Stetson sat forward on his head.

When he reached the walk in front of Longarm, he mounted the saloon's steps and paused beside him before entering. He had yellow hair and light skin blistered by the sun. When he glanced at Longarm, his green eyes glinted in the light pouring from the saloon behind Longarm.

"You Long?" the tall gent asked, his lips barely moving.

4

Longarm nodded.

"I'm Barton. Gil Forman is here, all right. Eat your supper, then I'll meet you in my hotel room later. Room 25, in back."

Barton brushed past Longarm and shouldered into the saloon. Longarm was about to leave the porch and cross to the hotel when he saw the rider who had trailed him from Sheridan City clop past. He was a short man with a heavy brush of a mustache and thick, tousled hair that came to his shoulders. At Sheridan City's train depot, this same man had been lounging idly by the baggage cart, waiting for someone to arrive, apparently a deputy U.S. marshal who had come all the way from Denver.

Both rider and horse were pale as ghosts from alkali dust. The rider did not flick a single glance in Longarm's direction. But there was no doubt in Longarm's mind that the rider had seen him and noted his presence on the saloon porch. In a moment the alkali-covered rider had disappeared into the street's gloom farther on toward the canyon, and Longarm found his cheroot had gone out.

After lighting up the cheroot again, Longarm crossed the street to the hotel, signed the register, and climbed a set of squeaking stairs to a room on the second floor facing the main street. He put his cheroot down carefully on the corner of the low dresser, took off his coat and shirt, and filled the washbowl from the pitcher. As soon as his big rough hands applied the soap and water to his face, he felt the sudden cracking of the alkali dust, like a mask crumbling, and tough though his face was, the soap burned its scorched surface. It had sure as hell been a hot day.

Suddenly unwilling to wait until the next day to rid himself of the trail's grime, he stripped, took a small hip flask of Maryland rye from his saddlebag and poured it into the bowl, cutting it only slightly with water. Then, with his bandanna, he gave himself as thorough a whore's bath as he could. The rye caused his skin to tingle some, and he felt a whole hell of a lot better, thinking for sure now he would make it through to the next day when he could soak in a barber's hot tub.

The deputy U.S. marshal's shoulders were broad, his shanks lean, and there was not an ounce of tallow on his tightly muscled waist. The raw sun and cutting winds of the many trails he had followed through the years since he left West-by-God-Virginia had cured his face and neck to saddle-leather brown. His eyes were gunmetal blue, set wide over high cheekbones. Only the tobacco-leaf shade of his close-cropped hair and longhorn mustache gave sure sign of his ancestry. Otherwise he might have passed for a full-blooded Indian.

Toweling himself dry, he stepped into the fresh long johns he took from his war bag, then put on a clean shirt as well, knotting a dark string tie at his throat. He slapped the dust off his brown pants and struggled back into them. Longarm wore them tight because he knew well the dangers of loose-fitting trousers, knew a sweat-soaked fold of cloth or leather between a rider and his mount could raise a blister in less than an hour. His fly buttoned, he pulled on his low-heeled cavalry stove-pipes. Longarm spent as much time afoot as in the saddle, and in these boots he could run with surprising speed.

After buttoning up his brown vest, he dropped his

6

double-barreled .44 derringer into its fob pocket, then draped the gold chain clipped to it across his chest to his watch. Next he slipped on his waxed, heat-hardened cross-draw rig containing his Colt Model T .44-40, and slapping the dust off his brown frock coat, shrugged into it. When he planted his snuff-brown Stetson slightly forward on his head and snugged it into place, he felt considerably more civilized and left his room to get something to eat.

Downstairs in the hotel's dining room he found a table, ordered his meal, and sat back with all his muscles loose, fully enjoying the luxury that followed a long ride. This one, from Sheridan City, had lasted two days and the last half day of it—spent crossing that blistering stove top of a desert—had made him feel like a board that had lain out in the sun too long, brittle and maybe a mite warped. His meal came and he ate it with gusto, ordered more coffee, then sat back and lit his second cheroot. He was trying to quit, but, lacking a woman, a man had to have some vices to comfort him.

He was about to leave for his appointment with Barton when he saw a strikingly handsome woman pause in the dining room doorway. Something in the way she let her eyes sweep the room, her cool imperiousness, caught Longarm's attention, the strength in her drawing him like a magnet. Though every bit a mature woman, she was still young, with black hair and a lush, full ripeness to her upper body that riveted him. At the moment, her lips, full and passionate, were set with iron resolve, her manner coolly indifferent to the gaze of so many men looking over from their tables.

She left the doorway and moved toward him, taking

a table on the other side of his, a woman eating alone, but doing so without pause or reflection on that fact. As she sat down, he kept his gaze boldly on her. Catching his glance, she did not look away, as direct in her own gaze as he was in his. Her eyes were black-gray and her hands small and square as they rested on the table. She knew she was beautiful and framed her picture for his glance, and those of every other man in that dining room. She did not so much delight in this as expect it, almost as a right. Her assurance was almost arrogant, and Longarm knew that few men had even been able to match the bold, open challenge she presented, and that too aroused him.

He wished his business in this place did not make it impossible for him to know this woman.

Signing his check, he left the dining room and moved up the stairs to the third floor, found his way down a dim hallway to room 25, and knocked. There was no answer. He knocked again, then tried the door. It was locked. He was too early, then. Frowning slightly, he moved back to his own room and dropped onto the bed, crossing his arms behind his back while he gave Seth Barton a chance to get to his room. After a good fifteen minutes he left his room again and knocked a second time on room 25. When he got no response, he became irritated, then nervous.

Back in his room, he spent a while pacing until he heard a sudden uproar from the saloon across the street. He went to the window and was just in time to see two wildly swinging men spill out of the saloon and into the street. Longarm cursed aloud.

Seth Barton was one of the two struggling men.

The other man was an oversized bully dressed in a logger's wool hat and jacket, and resembled more a bull buffalo than a human. After them came a noisy crowd, urging on the two combatants with wild, shrill cries. Nothing so pleased a crowd as the sight of someone else's blood. Grunts of surprise and even approval sprang from the encircling crowd as Barton managed to get in a few licks. Even so, it was clear to Longarm and to everyone in the crowd that the big logger would have no problem disposing of the far more slightly built man.

Barton was obviously no longer under cover, and this fight was sure as hell no accident, coming as it did so soon after Longarm's arrival. Longarm left his room, plunged down the stairs out of the hotel, and bulled his way through the crowd. Barton was twisting on the ground by then, while the logger kicked him repeatedly in the ribs with his steel-toed boots. Longarm grabbed the logger by the arm and swung him around. The logger flung up his forearms in surprise, managing to ward off Longarm's first punch. Longarm felt his clenched fist slam into the fellow's huge, meaty branch of an arm, the shuddering recoil traveling clear to his shoulder. Grinning, the giant advanced on Longarm, who promptly took a few quick steps back to give himself room.

As he did so, he felt the ground-trembling thunder of hoofbeats. Glancing over his shoulder, he saw the crowd melting swiftly away before a solid phalanx of mounted men, riding abreast as they swept down the street. The gang was charging directly at Longarm and Seth Barton. One of the riders in the first rank was the man who had followed Longarm from Sheridan City.

No longer interested in either Seth Barton or Longarm, the big man turned about and raced for the safety of the boardwalk, the crowd surging after him, leaving Barton and Longarm to the oncoming riders' plunging hooves.

Rushing to Barton's side, Longarm grabbed him under the armpits and began to drag him out of the street. But he did not have the time. The tide of horsemen was almost on him. Drawing his .44, he fired up at the closest rider. The shot went high, and before he could get off another one the storm of hooves was on him. He flung himself toward the sidewalk. A horse flashed past, its chest slamming Longarm's shoulder, the force of it enough to send him spinning violently into an alley's dark entrance. His head struck the hard, unyielding surface of an outside stairway. Groggy, he pulled himself up in time to see the riders wheeling back around now, coming after him. He managed to lift the Colt, but it seemed to weigh a ton. His hand shook as he tried to level it.

A woman grabbed him from behind and yanked him down the alley. A second later he was pulled up onto a back porch, a door was opened, and he went stumbling into a small kitchen. He turned to see the woman he had noticed in the hotel dining room slam the kitchen door shut behind her.

"No more heroics, mister. Keep your head down. Let me handle this."

She snatched up a Greener leaning in a corner and turned to face the door. Heavy boots tramped up onto the small porch and fists hammered on the door.

"You got him in there, Kate?"

"What if I have, Clem?"

"Damn you! He's a lawman!"

"Get off my porch or I'll blow a hole in you!"

The pounding came again. "Kate! I'm warning you!"

"And I'm warning you. This here Greener's loaded with double-aught buckshot. It'll tear a hole in this door and you besides. They'll have to pick you off that wall behind you."

"You're bluffin', Kate!"

She stepped to the window and blew it out with one barrel, sending shards of glass and pieces of shattered window sash exploding into the alley. Then, as the echo of the powerful detonation died, she stepped back in front of the door.

"I ain't goin' to tell you again, Clem!" she told him, her voice resonant with resolve.

That announcement was unnecessary. Heavy boots clattered down the porch steps, and a moment later Longarm heard the man she had called Clem yelling to his riders to saddle up. There were a few shouts, followed by the clatter of departing horses. As the men rode out of town, someone sent a round into the night sky out of sheer exuberance. Then came silence, a hushed, waiting silence broken only by a few distant shouts, queries.

Longarm slumped into a chair, his head buzzing, and thought of Seth Barton's trampled figure lying out there in the street. Then he grabbed hold of the table and sank his head down on it, aware for the first time of a huge gash in the side of his head, its warm blood trickling down his neck.

Only dimly was he aware of the woman yanking him upright, then steering his tall frame through a bedroom doorway. The last thing he remembered was lying on his back on a bed while the woman wrapped a towel around his head and cursed off his tight britches.

Chapter 2

The sun spilling into the bedroom caused Longarm's head to ache. He squinted up at Kate, a crooked grin on his face. She had a tray in her hand, a platter of fried eggs and bacon with thick slabs of buttered toast. Real butter. And a tall mug of coffee. He took the coffee off the tray as she set it down on the nightstand.

"I'll finish off that platter out in the kitchen," he told her, carefully sipping the scalding coffee. "Soon as I get dressed and washed up some." Then he became aware of the bandage wrapped about his head and reached up to feel of it. He frowned. "How long've I been here?"

"Two days."

"Must have been a nuisance. Sorry."

"No apologies needed."

"What about Seth Barton?"

"The man fighting with Bull?"

He nodded.

"He's torn up badly. Two broken ribs at least and a crushed hip. He'll live, but he won't be getting around so good after this."

"Jesus."

"That wasn't who did it."

"Where's Barton now, who's taking care of him?"

"Doc Wolfson. He's got an office over the barbershop and some spare beds in a back room. I trust him. Barton will be safe up there."

"Who's paying the doc?"

"I am."

"That's right decent of you." Longarm closed his eyes. What little he had seen of the Utah deputy he had liked. But he had been careless. And it had cost him. And almost cost Longarm, too. He took a deep breath and looked over at Kate, an inquiring frown on his face.

"I heard hammering," he told her. "Coming from the kitchen."

"That's what woke you up?"

Longarm nodded.

"Carpenters fixing my window. The Greener did considerable damage."

"I remember," Longarm said, nodding. "But not too clearly."

She picked up the tray and started for the door. "Finish your coffee and get freshened up if you want. Your clothes are over there on the chair. And your weapons. I think that vest-pocket derringer of yours is cute."

"Comes in handy sometimes."

"I can imagine." She paused with one hand on the doorknob. "I'll be waiting in the dining room. The carpenters are still in the kitchen, putting in the glass."

"All right, Kate."

She smiled and left him.

Kate had placed a silver cover over the platter so that
the eggs and bacon were not dried out. It wouldn't have
mattered if they had been. Longarm was famished and
ate eagerly, filling a hunger that had grown to the size of
the Grand Canyon. His head ached slightly, but he paid
it no attention.

The woman's full name was Kate Summerfield, and
it turned out she owned The Owl Hoot saloon, the hotel,
the feed mill, and a general store, all of them acquired
at various times in payment for gambling debts. She had
asked Longarm for one of his cheroots, and was smoking it now. His breakfast done, Longarm lit his own and
sat back in the high-backed, cushioned chair.

"You knew I was a lawman, Kate," he told her, "the
moment you caught sight of me in that restaurant. That
right?"

"Seth was a nice enough fellow," she replied. "But
he was very bad at keeping secrets. Everyone knew
what he was doing in town. And God knows how many
of Forman's gang saw him pause on the saloon's porch
last night to speak to you." She smiled wryly at Barton's
lack of good sense. "And you were only the second
stranger in town in three weeks."

"Well, he'll have plenty of time to think on that now.
Who was the rider who tracked me from Sheridan
City?"

She laughed, exhaling a cloud of smoke. "Frank
Tyson. Matt Forman sent him to the station to see who

Seth Barton was waiting for. The telegrapher at the depot in Sheridan City is Frank Tyson's brother."

"So when Seth telegraphed Billy Vail in Denver, Gil Forman and his brother knew that telegram's contents."

Kate nodded. "That's right. Even got your name. And when Frank Tyson rode in right after you, the party was on. For the past three days Forman's men had been drifting into town waiting for this."

"I'm sorry to put you in the middle of all this, Kate."

"That's where I've always been. That's where this town sits, between the hill ranchers and the big cattlemen beyond the range. Since I own most of this town, it serves everyone's best interest to let me and the town alone." She paused, her brows knitting. "Besides, Matt Forman's asked me to marry him. And I just might."

"You mean you're thinking about it."

She smiled, a cold light gleaming in her eyes. "Matt's finally swallowed his pride enough to make an offer to a gambling woman who owns the best saloon in town, along with a fine stable of clean . . . dancers. It took a while for him to come around, but he's done so."

"Sticking your neck out for me might mess things up between you two."

"Matt would be a fool to let that happen. And if he's that much of a fool, I don't want him."

"You sure you do anyway, Kate?"

She sighed. "Comes a time when a woman's got to make the best deal she can. I think maybe that time is near."

"Getting near, maybe. But it ain't here yet. Not from where I'm sitting right now."

"Nice of you to say that."

"I mean it."

"I know you do, Custis. Listen, can you take good advice when you hear it? Make tracks from this place — and fast. I know Matt. He has no intention of letting you bring in his kid brother."

"Gil Forman killed a young girl in Denver, the daughter of a local lawman. I knew him, and the girl. So did Marshal Vail."

Kate frowned. "Talk hereabouts is Gil was framed, then released without being charged."

"They had to release him. Lack of evidence."

"And now?"

"We found the evidence that would have convicted him. But we found it too late, after he left Denver."

Frowning, she leaned forward. "My God, Custis, what *was* the evidence?"

"You don't need to know, Kate."

She leaned back in her chair. "Then I think I should warn you. This far from Denver, you won't get much help from the local law. The town marshal and the sheriff are both in Forman's back pocket. Bought and paid for."

"That fact was in Seth's telegram."

"But aren't you way out of your jurisdiction? This here's Montana Territory. I'll bet you don't even have a warrant."

"No, I don't. And if I brought Gil Forman back he would be tried in a local, Denver city court, not a federal court. But that doesn't matter. My chief, Billy Vail, is backing me on this."

17

"You just want Gil Forman. And you're willing to bend the rules some."

"This case is . . . special, Kate. It would be criminal to let Gil Forman get away with what he did to that girl."

"The evidence is that damning, is it?"

"Yes, it is, Kate."

Her brows knitted, she nodded, satisfied. Then she stubbed out her smoke in a saucer.

Longarm got to his feet. "There's just one thing I really need," he said, smiling down at her, "before I move on out of here."

She got to her feet also. "And what might that be?"

"A good hot bath. I've been needing one since I rode in."

"There's a tub in the back room. I'll send over one of my girls to fill it. She'll even scrub your back, if you want."

He smiled down into her eyes. "I wish you'd take care of that," he told her.

"Well now," she said, brightening. "That might be arranged."

He stepped toward her. She did not retreat. Her lips were slightly apart, glistening with moisture. It would take but a nudge to open them. She had to lift her head to meet his gaze, and suddenly her eyes were heavy with longing. He saw want, deep and powerful, flood into them. He put his hands on her hips and nudged her closer until her full thighs pressed against his. Then he kissed her full on the lips, and found them opening with a warmth and urgency that stirred his groin to life.

Her eyes grew darker as she pushed him gently away.

18

The self-confidence in them grew oddly bitter. "You did that easily enough. But I warn you, Custis Long, I am not easy. Not to any man."

"I didn't think you were."

There was a power of hatred in her and he felt it burning in her now. The intensity of it shocked him. But it did not repel him. If anything, it only made her all the more desirable.

He smiled amiably down at her, refusing to take offense. "Back at that restaurant I was sorry I wouldn't be seeing you again. I'm glad it didn't work out that way, despite this sore head."

She took a step closer. "Kiss me again," she told him, the anger in her voice gone. "Then I'll get the water for your bath. And maybe I'll take a bath, too."

"I'd like that."

"Kiss me, damn you," she said. "And shut up."

He took her in his arms and did as she bid.

They were both still damp when they struck the silken coverlet of her large, canopied bed. They had been playing some during the bath, and when they came to rest on the bed they were both feverish with their need.

She pulled him down to her. He kissed her with a hungry savagery, his lips pressing her mouth open wider. He sent his tongue darting in boldly and felt her pull back in surprise, like a startled deer that finds more than a handful of grass waiting at its nose. But the hesitation gave way to desire and she answered his thrusting tongue eagerly, wantonly.

Pulling back from the kiss momentarily, he grinned down at her as he gazed upon her lush ripeness. But she would have no pause now and pulled him down onto her breasts with a fierceness that amused him, thrusting one of her breasts into his mouth. He took her nipple in his mouth and let his tongue encircle the flat tip, then flick it repeatedly until it came fully to attention, allowing him to enclose it gently but firmly between his teasing teeth. She gasped and her arms tightened convulsively about his shoulders.

He pushed himself atop her and let his throbbing shaft nudge against her moist, silken muff. Her arms tightened about his back as she opened her thighs to him. In he plunged, driving hard and deep. A delighted gasp broke from her and he felt her nails raking his back. Still thrusting deeply, he leaned back enough to grab one of her breasts in his big hand and squeeze. A sudden glow suffused her face.

"No more play!" she told him, almost angrily. "Give it to me!"

Obedient to her cry—and to his own needs—he did as she pleaded, and in a moment was no longer thinking of her, but only of his own urgency as he pounded into her. She bucked under him, her head thrashing from side to side, no longer bothering to rake his back—like him, intent only on crossing that barrier—until at last she cried out unashamedly and they plunged over it together and were lost in the hot urgency of their mutual spasms.

When it was done for him, he let himself sag forward onto her warm lushness, panting slightly, aware of the rosy glow that warmed her face and the fine patina of moisture that covered her milk-white shoulders and breasts.

"You had enough, Kate?"

"Don't ask foolish questions. Someday I'll meet a man who won't roll over and start snoring on me."

"Maybe you already have."

"Show me."

He leaned back and gazed upon her. She let him, making no effort at all to pull a sheet over her. "Just let me look first. That helps, you know."

She looked back at him just as boldly. "I don't mind. A woman likes to feel a man's eyes on her nakedness. It's something we need as much as you do."

It was still difficult for him to believe the ripeness of her, the silken, ample breasts, her narrow waist and flaring hips, in the valley of which rested the dark mystery of her gleaming, triangular nap. It was no wonder every man in that dining room had been unable to look away as she entered.

"Finished?" she asked.

"You mean am I ready."

"You know what I mean."

He rested his hand on her triangular patch, then let his fingers nudge past the moistness and slip inside.

"Hurry up, damn you, Custis," she told him, her voice heavy with urgency. "I can't wait any longer!"

He swung onto her once more, his thrusting erection sinking deep into her hot, moist warmth. With an exultant cry, she sucked him in still deeper. Amazed at her swift readiness, he hung back and looked down at her, a teasing smile on his face.

"You sure you're ready for this?"

"Yes, damn you!" she hissed. "Yes!"

He drove hard into her, drew back, and drove in

21

again, each thrust punctuated by her deep, guttural gasps of pleasure. Every part of her body responded, her hot flesh beyond control now, her nails raking his back, her teeth clenched in a kind of frenzy as she tossed her head wildly back and forth.

Her wild gyrations almost caused him to lose his rhythm, but he kept to it and was soon caught up in her wildness. Her muted cries grew stronger, then shattered, her fingers digging into his legs, her body plunging upward, slamming hard against him. With the suddenness of a cougar's wail, a piercing shriek came from her, then trailed away into a long, soft moan. Longarm remained poised deep within her, the unbearable tension in his groin flashing suddenly, like gunpowder, ripping at him as he lunged still deeper for one more final, explosive thrust. Then he was expending himself within her throbbing warmth, a sudden, overpowering lassitude claiming him at last.

Piling down from the heights, he gazed deeply into her dark eyes and smiled.

"You all right, Kate?" he inquired.

"Oh, God," she moaned softly as she lay with her abdomen sucking in, then out, her body caught up in a delayed orgasm.

He pressed his cheek down on her warm breasts and waited for her to calm down. At last, with a deep sigh, her hand came down to caress his back and shoulder. It was then she felt the long ridges her nails had left.

"My poor dear, have I torn up your back?"

"I'll live."

As he pulled gently back, she turned in his arms and

pulled his face close to hers, kissing him hungrily, her lips soft and pliant.

"Thank you, Custis. That was lovely."

"You see, I didn't roll over and go to sleep."

"No, you didn't, and that's a fact." She patted his head gingerly. "How's that nasty gash?"

"No bother."

"Good. I wouldn't want that to slow you down any."

"You mean you ain't finished yet?"

She laughed softly. "Of course not."

"Do your damnedest," he told her. "I'll hope for the best."

With a soft, deep laugh, she moved on top of him, prowling over him like a big cat, her molten lips enclosing his. Gently, she eased back until she found his growing erection and with swift fingers guided him once more into her. With an explosive sigh, she eased herself slowly back and sucked him in still deeper, smiling down at him from a great height, her hair spilling about him like a tent, a dark, fragrant tent. Astonishingly, he felt the hard barrel of his shaft thrusting deeper and still deeper into her.

Pleased at his resurrection, she laughed again, a deep, husky laugh. "You see what happens when I do my damnedest?"

"I'm still hoping," he told her.

She leaned her head back and began rocking back and forth. "Don't worry, Custis," she told him between clenched teeth.

He didn't, and it soon became obvious that he was going to have no trouble as the surging intensity of their lovemaking increased. Reaching up, he cupped her breasts in his own big hands and let the wildness come again, losing himself completely in its savage intensity until at last he and Kate climaxed. Kate let herself collapse forward onto the bed beside him.

This time they were both entirely spent, long-distance runners who had just crossed the finish line. Firmly clasped in each other's arms, they drifted off, and the last thing Longarm remembered was thinking how hungry he had become once again.

Chapter 3

As Longarm ate his second meal of the day, Kate pitched in beside him. He got the distinct impression he had passed muster with this formidable woman. He had even caught her humming a tune earlier in the kitchen as she prepared the meal. Now, with their coffee mugs sitting before them on the table, Longarm thanked Kate.

"It's a pleasure to cook for a real man," she told him. "Besides, you needed it. I wouldn't want to weaken you any, especially when I think what you might be riding into."

"Give me a picture of the situation around here, Kate. You mentioned hill people and cattlemen. It sounded like they were two warring groups."

"The hill ranchers run cattle, but their ranges are considerably smaller than the big spreads on the other side of this range."

"Why the conflict?"

"The big cattlemen say they're losing too much stock to the smaller ranchers in the hills."

"Are they?"

Kate shrugged. "Could be."

"Why don't the big cattlemen band together and stop it?"

"One of the cattlemen is trying to do that. His name is Tom Goodnight. But he's not having much success."

"Why not?"

"I think a lot of it has to do with the Big Burnout."

"What the hell's that?"

"About ten years ago a stretch of timber north of here caught fire, wiping out several logging camps and a couple of towns. Nobody heard much about it, I imagine. It didn't get the attention the Chicago fire got, that's for sure. But for the loggers and the people in those towns, it was pure hell, and there weren't many who escaped."

"What's that got to do with the hill ranchers and the cattlemen?"

"Give me a minute, Custis."

He sipped his coffee and grinned at her. "I'm listening."

"Would you like something to sweeten that?"

"You wouldn't happen to have any Maryland rye, would you?"

With a quick smile she left the table and returned with a bottle of Maryland rye, unstoppered the bottle, and placed it down beside Longarm.

"Thanks," he said, slugging the coffee. "Would you like another smoke?"

"I thought you'd never ask."

He took out two cheroots, lit hers and his own, then relaxed while she told him what she knew about the Big Burnout.

About ten years before, Kate explained, a forest fire wiped out close to a seventy-five-square-mile swath north of Placer Town. Probably getting its start in a slash pile near some logger's camp, the fire smoldered for a long while in the thick mat of pine duff under the taller timber, building up heat until, without warning, one dry fall afternoon it flashed into explosive fire within minutes, creating a crown fire that raced from treetop to treetop at express-train speed, sucking up into its flaming maw anything or anyone on the ground— men, women, children, horses, wagons, shacks, houses, and cut timber. Once the flames had consumed all the easy fuel high in the trees, they swept down the trunks, wiping out anything that remained, leaving finally only a smoking desolation of black, charred tree trunks, each one standing like a dismal tombstone in a vast wasteland of ash.

"You talk like you were there," Longarm remarked when Kate finished describing the fire.

"I was. I lost my father in the fire, and two younger brothers, along with all our family possessions. My pa got me out of it in time, and then went back for the others. I never saw him again. That fire left me an orphan."

"Well, you seem to have survived well enough."

Frowning slightly, she glanced out the window. "Whenever we get a long, hot summer, like this one, I begin to remember. That year, I don't think we got a drop of rain after the first week in June. When October came, that pine forest was tinder-dry, waiting to explode."

"There was another fire like the one you just described. In Peshtigo, Wisconsin. What year was the fire north of here?"

She told him.

"Yep. Same year. That must've been one hell of a dry year, all right."

"It was that."

He smiled and peered inquiringly at her. "Now, you going to tell me what the Big Burnout has to do with that cattle rustling you mentioned?"

"Those seventy-five square miles have grown back, after a fashion. And what they are now is a perfect badland, an ideal place for hiding rustled stock."

"How so?"

"It's a hellish tangle of hardwood saplings, ax-handle thick alders, and pines no taller than you or me. And if that isn't enough, the whole awful mess is tied together with shin-deep poison ivy, woodpine, deadly nightshade, and blackberry canes. I've ridden through it, or tried to, but the only way to go is to follow the bear paths and other game trails, if you can find any, and even they don't seem to lead anywhere. It's a treacherous maze, Custis. You can get hopelessly lost inside there, unless you really know it."

"And the hill ranchers know it."

"Some do, at any rate."

"And that's where the rustled cattle are being taken, and why the big cattlemen can't do much about it."

Kate shrugged. "That's what the talk here in town is.

And it's what I hear late at night around the card tables, when maybe too much whiskey gets drunk and the hill ranchers' tongues get to flapping."

"Is Matt Forman mixed up in any of this?"

"Matt assures me he's not." She sighed. "I'd like to believe it. But when I consider that crew of his, I'm pretty sure he's up to something. He has more men than he needs for the size of his spread. And there are times when his crew thins out, like most of them are off somewhere."

"You mean off driving rustled cattle to a buyer."

"Yes."

"You got any idea where that might be?"

"There's a town north of this range, near the border, a mining town. What I hear is buyers from Canada and Oregon will take any cattle a man can drive that far north, no questions asked."

"What's the name of the place?"

"Silver Creek."

Longarm puffed reflectively on his cheroot. It looked like he had dropped right into the middle of a range war. Even so, that changed little. What Matt Forman was up to was not Longarm's concern. He was here to bring in Gil Forman. "Can you steer me to Matt Forman's ranch?" he asked Kate.

"Keep on past the canyon. Stay on the road. It's deep into the hills. You'll see it at the end of a long flat."

"How long a ride is it?"

"Two days at least. It's steep, rough country, but even so, Matt's got some of the best graze in the hills. You can't miss his big log house. It sits high on a bluff."

"Thanks."

"You won't heed my warning?"

"You mean go back without Gil Forman?"

"Yes."

"Of course not."

"You're a stubborn man."

Longarm got to his feet. "Before I set out, I've got to see how Seth's doing."

Kate got up also. "I'll go with you."

Doc Wolfson was not a very impressive looking man of medicine. His sunken cheeks were rosy with the hectic flush of the consumptive. A nearly empty bottle of whiskey sat on his desk, a tin cup beside it. The office itself was a shambles.

Too disorganized to shake Longarm's hand when Kate introduced him, he mumbled something apologetic about the office's appearance and made a feeble effort to clear off his desk. Then, running long fingers through his thinning hair, he led Longarm and Kate into the room where the U.S. deputy marshal from Utah was recuperating. Barton did not look good. His face was still swollen from the beating he took from the logger, and his head and ribs were tightly bandaged. His back propped up by two large pillows, he was staring morosely out through a dirty window when Kate, followed by Longarm, entered the long attic room.

Longarm stopped by the cot. "How you feeling, Seth?"

"I've felt better. The doc here says my hip's broke."

"Along with a couple of ribs," Doc Wolfson said, stepping closer.

"What're you goin' to do now, Long?" Barton asked.

"Looks like I'm going to have to have a talk with Gil Forman's brother."

"Sure wish I could go with you."

"Stay put. Soon as I get back, we'll put you on a train."

"That can wait. Just get that bastard for me."

"It's Gil Forman I came for."

"I ain't forgettin' that," Barton replied, his voice raw with anger. "But it was Matt Forman who put me in this bed."

Longarm clapped Barton on the shoulder. "I won't be forgetting that, either, Seth."

Longarm looked up and nodded to Kate, then followed her and the doctor from the room.

"He'll be all right," the doc said, walking to the outer door with them. "He's been hurt bad, but I figure he'll be able to ride in a couple of weeks, maybe a month."

"I should be back in plenty of time to give him a hand, Doc. Meanwhile, take good care of him."

"If you need anything, Doctor," Kate said, "get in touch with me."

"All right, Kate."

Longarm clapped on his hat, left the office, and moved down the wooden steps outside with Kate. At the bottom, Kate paused to squint through the late-afternoon sunshine at Longarm.

"It's late. Do you really have to leave today?"

"I want to get on with this, Kate. I've already given Gil Forman too much time to think. He knows I'm here."

"He might kill you."

31

"If he does, he'll be killing a federal marshal. And there are a lot more where I came from. There'll be plenty of warrants then."

"Is it that important—that you bring Gil in, I mean?"

"Yes."

"You mentioned evidence before. I wish I knew what it was."

Longarm adjusted the saddlebags resting on his shoulder. "It's better you don't know. The evidence is not very pleasant—damn ugly, in fact."

"In my business, Custis, I've seen a lot you wouldn't call pleasant."

To end the argument, he said gently, "I'll be pushing off now. Thanks—for everything, Kate."

"You're as stubborn as a mule, Custis Long. But stubborn or not, I'll be looking forward to seeing you again."

He grinned. "And I'll sure be looking forward to another hot bath."

She kicked him in the shins, gently.

He didn't get far that day, as he knew he wouldn't, but he slept well enough under the stars. At the first light of a new day he set out, following the road all the way through the canyon, lifting out of it gradually until he came to a creek gushing violently down the mountainside. He crossed a gravel ford and, disregarding Kate's advice, left the road. Deep in the pines he built a small fire, cooked bacon and coffee, shaved, then resumed his journey.

The sun was high beyond the tops of the pines, the western slope up which he toiled still gray and cold.

There was almost no underbrush. The red pines crowded thickly about him, the almost solid mat of their branches trapping the shadowy pearl light of dawn long after full day lightened the sky. A thousand years of needle-fall made a spongy surface upon which the horse's feet dropped with scarcely a sound. Except for the slight jingle of the bridle metal and the occasional distant tap of a woodpecker's bill, a primeval stillness hung over the timbered slope.

Every now and then he passed over narrow cattle trails. Twice he came upon a wagon's course. He rode on without haste, stopping frequently to let the horse blow, and found himself thinking of Kate, and of her wish to know what the evidence was they had found after Gil Forman was released from custody. Longarm had brought the evidence, or part of it, with him. It was folded carefully in one of his two saddlebags—a pair of pink, lace-trimmed bloomers that had belonged to Aleta Crowley, the girl who would never see her eighteenth birthday. Discolored with her blood, the fabric of the undergarment was rent by two neat but powerful slashes of a long knife—the kind Gil owned. A Green River. A mountain-man's knife he put much store by, according to all reports.

By an odd chance, the girl's undergarments had found their way into Gil's laundry bag and had been cleaned and ironed along with the rest of his laundry, then wrapped and delivered to his room after he lit out. When the police stumbled upon this evidence, they turned Gil's quarters upside down and found the rest of the girl's torn and bloody garments rolled into a stiffened bundle, hidden inside an old cardboard suitcase Gil had rammed through a loose board in the back of his bedroom closet. Longarm and Billy Vail had hoped that once Gil's brother had a chance to consider this grisly evidence, he would be willing to cooperate with Longarm in apprehending his brother, even if with the greatest reluctance. But now Longarm was not so sure.

At noon he dismounted before another creek, rested, and resumed his way. After the first quick rise beyond the canyon, the mountain slopes began to break into benches where shortgrass meadows and finger-shaped valleys lay between the green patches of timber. He crossed these openly, still high above the road, reached timber, and climbed again to the next, higher bench. The road suddenly swung around toward him. Thus far the timber had furnished good traveling, but at this point the steep slopes began to break into canyons and sharp-backed ridges, through which the road made the only comfortable passage.

He took it, and sunset found him camped beside a creek just above it. He picketed his horse in a small flat and made his meal. Then he built up the fire larger than he needed, drew his blankets beyond the fire's glow and watched the world plunge into darkness. Against the black heavens swarms of stars flickered, beckoning to him. He felt the earth turning under him as a gentle wind, chilled at this elevation, brushed his cheek. What light there was came from a thin sliver of a moon tilted low to the southwest.

He was not far from the road and could just make out its pale surface below him. Somewhere there would be ranch quarters, and at some time or another travelers would pass and see his fire, which was his intention. He smoked a cheroot contentedly, enjoying the ease that comes after a long day's journey. When he heard the run of a horse far down the road, he turned in his blanket and threw a handful of pine needles on the fire. The blaze crackled and lifted its light against the darkness.

He listened to the horse come on as he had listened to the like sound on many another night in many another place, interest and caution rising together. He lay flat on his back, his head against his saddle and his feet to the fire. The rider came quickly around a bend in the road, reached a point abreast of him, and stopped. He saw the rider's shape bend in the saddle and straighten up again. He heard the squeak of saddle leather as a woman's voice came to him out of the darkness.

"Hello!"

She sat still on the sidesaddle. In the dim moonlight he could barely make out her tan shirt and long, dark riding skirt, and a man's hat sitting back on hair the color of dark honey. He said hello back at her, and she rode up the grade until she got close enough for him to see the graceful curve of her neck as she craned to see beyond the leaping fire.

"You don't make sense, mister."

"What kind of sense you looking for, ma'am?"

"You keep away from the road all day, as if you were on the run. Then you camp here where everybody can see you, and build a fire big as a house. And now you keep yourself back in the shadows so a body can't get a look at you."

She was nervous, he realized, and was really asking if maybe he had a gun trained on her. "Relax," he told

35

her sitting up. "And tell me how you know I kept off the road."

"I saw you a while back and followed, from a safe distance, of course."

"Why?"

"I was curious."

"That's no answer, but let that go for now."

"You didn't think you could ride this far into these hills without anyone noticing, did you?"

"I'm not on the run, if that's what's bothering you."

Longarm got slowly to his feet. He saw her stiffen some as she took note of his tall figure. He smiled, a white streak against the shadows of his face, the fire throwing into sharp relief its rugged planes. Her eyes narrowed in quick appraisal. She seemed pleased with what she saw.

"This is no place to camp," she told him. "You'd get a bullet in that fire before another hour had passed."

"What do you suggest?"

"It's too dangerous for a stranger out here. Saddle up and come to our ranch."

"And what ranch might that be?"

"Sun Ranch."

He saw her eyes narrow suddenly as she got a better look at him and realized there was something in his appearance that told her who he was. "Are you the one who tried to stop Bull Bronson from beating up that deputy marshal the other night?"

Longarm nodded. "That's the logger's name? Bronson?"

"Yes. And usually in Matt Forman's employ whenever Matt needs a Neanderthal to do his bidding."

"I didn't do too well."

"That's no wonder. My father was in town when it happened. He told me about it. No one has ever been able to stop Bronson."

The rapid drumming of horses' hooves suddenly filled the night. They were coming from the west.

"Saddle up and kick out the fire," the girl said impatiently.

Longarm made up his blanket roll in quick turns, threw on the saddle and lashed his roll. He gave the fire a quick, sideways kick with his boot, sending the blazing firewood into the stream.

Mounting up, he let her take the lead as she moved ahead of him up the slope. At the top of the grade they crossed a narrow flat and kept on into the timber, leaving the road behind. Presently, deep in the woods, she halted and they sat their horses, listening. A moment later a storm of horsemen swept past them in the night.

"They'll be at the ranch waiting for us," she told him.

"Then let's go," he said.

They descended to the road and kept on it through a shallow canyon, still rising into the cool night. Reaching a level area surrounded by the shadow of ragged hills, they crossed a creek making a swift, smooth run across their paths. Lights gleamed ahead as a door opened and Longarm saw shapes cut in front of them, moving across a yard, the riders that had plunged out of the night behind them earlier. A plank bridge boomed a warning of their approach, and soon they were approaching a log house built low and long across the yard. Four sweaty horses were standing at the hitch rack, their tails drooping wearily.

The huge, square shape of a man stood in the lighted doorway, peering out at them. They pulled to a halt in front of the low porch and dismounted. The big man moved out onto the porch. Stepping through the doorway after him came another man—tall, slim, his square face clean-shaven, his eyes cold. He wore his arrogance like a badge.

Longarm was finally going to meet Matt Forman.

As Longarm and the woman approached the porch steps, three other men crowded out onto the porch after Matt Forman. One of them was Gil Forman, a smaller, meaner version of his older brother. Longarm recognized him at once; he had been on hand when Gil Forman had been brought in for questioning after the discovery of Aleta's battered corpse.

The woman said, "I picked this man up on the road, Dad. He wanted a sleep and a meal."

The big, blocky man brushed past Matt Forman to the edge of the porch to peer down at Longarm. "My name's Buckman, mister. And that's my daughter Ellen just brought you in. What's your name?"

"Custis Long."

"You in these hills to cause trouble, are you?"

Longarm glanced over at Matt Forman, then let his gaze slide on to Gil Forman. "If I don't get any trouble," he announced laconically, "I don't see why I should cause any."

"Fair enough," pronounced Buckman. He glanced at his daughter. "Show him the bunkhouse, Ellen. You done right. Strangers are welcome. Take him to the cookhouse when he's settled and see he gets a cup of coffee."

"Hold it right there, Buckman," Matt Forman snapped. "Maybe you believe what this stranger claims, but I know what he's doin' here. He's a lawman—come all the way from Denver to bring in Gil."

Buckman swung around to look at Longarm, a bit more closely this time. "That right, mister?"

"Right enough."

"You got a warrant for Gil—anything besides a badge, that is?"

"No."

"Well, then. You're still welcome to the bunk and the coffee, but I suggest you move on first thing in the morning. It would be better for all concerned."

"You got something to hide, Buckman?"

"Ain't a man livin' don't have *something* to hide, mister. You knowed that was a silly question when you asked it."

"Maybe it was at that."

Ellen waited outside the barn while Longarm stabled his horse, then walked him over to the bunkhouse.

"Dad's a good man, Mr. Long," Ellen said, her soft voice low. "But he's had a long life. And there's things he's done back there he'd probably just as soon forget. But I love him and I know that all he wants now is to live in peace and do what's right, so things will go well for me."

"I'm not after your father, Ellen."

"What's Gil done?"

39

"The law will decide that when I bring him back to stand trial."

"You said you didn't have a warrant."

"That's right."

"Then you're going to have to go against the law—and you're a lawman."

"I'm going to have to do what is necessary."

"Then watch out. Matt Forman is a ruthless man, and so is Gil. I don't like either of them. You saw them when we rode up. They were off their horses and into my father's house looking for you without a *by-your-leave*. Then they moved out onto our porch like it was their own. My father hates them, but there's nothing he can do to stop them. They're powerful and take what they want. In these dark hills, the owner of the Lazy M is king."

Frowning, Longarm glanced back at the ranch house. "Then I guess it took some guts for your father to offer his hospitality just now, and yours to bring me here in the first place. Once you got a good look at me, you knew who I was, and who you and your father would be going against. That right?"

They had reached the bunkhouse by this time. Ellen paused in front of it. "Yes," she said, gazing calmly up at him, "I knew. The truth is that we've been hearing things up here ever since that deputy from Utah rode into Placer Town. You wouldn't tell me what Gil's done. But most of us have a pretty good idea what he's been accused of doing." She sighed deeply, wearily. "You might say it's not out of character for the likes of Gil Forman."

40

'It's going to strengthen my hand some to know that, Ellen. Thanks."

"Now get settled inside," she told him. "If Abe's awake, have him take you to the cookshack. Good night, Mr. Long."

"Good night, Ellen."

Abe was a bent, white-haired old cowpoke, who had obviously ridden too many broncs in his time. After Longarm found himself a bunk, Abe put his teeth back in and escorted Longarm over to the cookshack. He left Longarm in the care of a very tall cook, whose sunken, cadaverous appearance made Longarm wonder immediately about the quality of the food provided for this ranch's crew.

The coffee was excellent, however, and Longarm was leaning against the open cookshack doorway, lighting up a cheroot, when Matt, Gil Forman, and their two hands walked over to deal with him. Longarm was not surprised. He had been expecting this visit.

Forman pulled to a halt in front of Longarm. "Get a good rest tonight, lawman. 'Cause you'll be starting a long ride in the morning."

"Yeah? How far *is* the Lazy M?"

"That ain't the direction you'll be taking. Fact is, you'll be riding right on through Placer Town, all the way back to Sheridan City."

"Sure, I'll go back, Forman. But not alone."

Gil Forman stepped closer, both fists doubled up at his sides, his thin, drawn face pale. "Why're we wastin' our time talkin' to this bastard?" he demanded through clenched teeth. "Let me take him right now, Matt."

41

"Shut up, Gil. I'll handle this.'

"Then handle it, damn you!"

Matt swung around and slapped Gil so hard the younger man stumbled back, his eyes tearing from the blow, his step unsteady. It looked for a second that he might spring on his brother in retaliation, but he swallowed his anger and contented himself with glaring balefully back at him.

"I won't tell you this again, Gil," Matt said coldly. "You don't ever tell me what to do. Ever." He turned then to direct his hard, furious gaze on Longarm. "And sure as hell not in front of this pile of coon shit."

"What's the problem, Forman," Longarm drawled, stepping away from the doorjamb. "Is there any reason why your brother shouldn't be willing to go back with me for a fair trial?"

"Don't get cute with me. We know what you're up to, mister. And so do you. You ain't got any legal right to take my brother anywhere. So I'm telling you plain. Ride out of here tomorrow and go back where you came from—or take my warning. These hills have swallowed a lot of secrets in the years past. One more won't crowd them none."

He turned quickly about then, and with his brother and the other two hands, headed back to their waiting horses. In a few minutes Longarm heard the four men gallop off into the night.

They had come after Longarm in Placer Town, but had missed him there. When they overtook him in the hills, he was up here in Buckman's place. If just now Matt Forman had not dealt with him as his brother wanted, it was only because Matt realized that Sun

42

Ranch had too many witnesses, and few if any of them could be bought off.

So Matt Forman would have to wait until the only witnesses would be those who gunned Longarm down.

Chapter 4

Longarm ate breakfast in the cookshack with the Sun Ranch crew, and when he finished he moved out into the mountain's bright morning light, into its thin, bracing air. After meeting with Buckman, the rest of the crew crossed the yard and were soon astride their mounts, moving into the trees, downgrade.

Ellen appeared on the front porch, caught sight of Longarm and descended the steps, heading toward him. She was wearing her long riding skirt and carrying a riding crop. When she reached him she asked if he had appreciated spending the night under a roof.

"The stars aren't all that bad."

She laughed. "Saddle up and ride with me," she said, moving on past him to the barn.

Longarm retrieved his gear from the bunkhouse, entered the barn and saddled his horse, then led it out.

Ellen was already up on her horse. Longarm stepped into his saddle and pulled alongside her, and they set off across a short mountain meadow, heading east. A road split the meadow. They followed it and presently reached timber, slipping into its cool morning twilight, going steadily upgrade.

"Where does this road go?" he asked.

"Over the mountains. East and beyond."

"Wrong direction, Ellen. I'm staying on the road, heading north, for the Lazy M, and Gil Forman."

"They won't be there."

"What are you trying to tell me, Ellen?"

"My father told me this morning. He didn't say I should let you know. He left that to me. Anyway, he overheard Matt Forman making plans. He and his crew are waiting up here in this timber somewhere, waiting for you to ride out of Sun Ranch. The way they're planning it, you'll just disappear somewhere in these hills."

Longarm looked quickly around. He saw no waiting horsemen in the trees, but that meant nothing. There was no reason not to believe Ellen was telling him the truth. It sounded like just what Matt Forman and his brother would do. Hell, it made good sense.

"Listen to me," Ellen went on. "East of here on the other side of this range there's a cattleman, Tom Goodnight. Tell him I sent you."

"You trust him, do you?'

"He wants to marry me."

"You agreeable to the idea?"

"I would be, if it weren't for Dad. But Dad wouldn't hear of it."

"Why not?"

"Pride more than anything else. When Dad first came to these hills, he was hardscrabble, nothing on his back and a past not worth mentioning. So he built a cabin out of logs he cut with a hand ax and rustled cattle to give himself a start."

"And the cattle he rustled belonged to Tom Goodnight."

"Yes. Though Dad only took enough to give himself a start, he still feels bad about it. It don't matter that Tom Goodnight's long since forgiven Dad the few mavericks he took. He still can't look Tom in the face. He's got this stubborn pride."

"Ellen, I wouldn't give a soggy cheroot for a man without pride, but sometimes it makes things a mite difficult."

"It surely does," she agreed somberly.

Reaching the crest of the grade up which their horses had been laboring, Ellen and Longarm halted, and she pointed to a tall pine atop a distant ridge. Blackened by a lightning bolt, it stood out starkly against the sky. "When you reach that pine look southeast to a long flat. Keep on across the flat through a narrow pass. It's the only way through this range without keeping on the road. On the other side of the pass, you'll come to Tom Goodnight's Circle T spread."

"You mean I'm to make a run for Goodnight's ranch."

"Yes. It's not much help, but it's all I can offer."

"I don't like the idea of running from Matt Forman and his crew. It sure as hell ain't very dignified."

"There's that fool male pride again."

Longarm chuckled. "I suppose so."

"Tom Goodnight will help you. He hates Matt Forman almost as much as my father does." She appraised him coolly. "Why not give Tom a chance to help you? He'll appreciate it."

"All right, then. Thanks, Ellen. And thank your father for me, too."

"Good luck, and say hello to Tom for me."

"I'll do that," he told her.

Touching his hat brim to her, he continued on across the ridge to the pine Ellen had pointed out to him, then pulled up and took the time to look back the way he and Ellen had come. Ellen was no longer in sight, and he saw no sign of pursuit on the trail they had followed. Not yet, anyway.

He turned back around and kept on down the long, steep slope until he reached the flat Ellen had indicated. Pulling up, he studied the distant pass, mentally computing his distance from it. A ride straight across the flat would leave him in plain sight for a long, long time, and the timbered slopes bordering the flat would hide any pursuit. He would be in plain sight for a long time, while Matt Forman and his riders would be out of sight in the timber, closing in.

He clapped spurs to his horse, but instead of cutting straight across the flat to the pass, he stayed close to the timber bordering the flat for close to a mile, then cut into one of the timbered foothills, booting his mount up it until he came upon a rocky shelf poking out of the trees and brush. Dismounting, he tethered the horse in under the shelf, unlimbered his Winchester, and ran farther up the slope until he gained a spot high enough to give him a clear view of the flat, clear to the pass beyond.

47

He didn't have long to wait.

Down through the timbered slopes Longarm had just left, a small band of riders poured. Sweeping out onto the flat, they plunged across it, heading for the pass. Once Forman and his gang had realized Longarm was not staying on the road heading north to the Lazy M, they had come back for him. They might have caught sight of Ellen, perhaps, coming from the east, and knew he was taking the only other route he could from the range. Now they were trying to overtake him before he got through the pass.

Watching them sweep across the flat toward the pass, Longarm returned to his horse, and booting it up the slope, found a ridge and kept along it, heading for the pass, his eye on the horsemen racing ahead of him across the flat. Keeping on until a wall of white rock blocked his way, he followed along its base to the flat, but kept in the timber, waiting for the Lazy M riders to vanish through the pass.

When they had, he rode out onto the flat and followed the trail until he came out onto the long, flat, gently sloping plains beyond it. In the distance he saw the clot of riders vanishing to the northeast. He cut due east, heading across the broad, sweeping grassland, the lush grass belly high. He had not gone far when he heard shouts and glanced to the north. A sharp-eyed rider had caught sight of him and the rest of the Lazy M crew were turning to come after him. Longarm bent low over his mount and gave it its head, and before long he caught sight of what he assumed was Tom Goodnight's ranch buildings on a slight rise, a timbered ridge at their back.

He was racing through a long, low swale when from

around a low knoll ahead of him four riders poured, charging directly toward him. Longarm hoped this might be Tom Goodnight's crew, but even if it were not, he saw that he had no choice but to keep on, and was soon halting before the lead rider, who came to a halt circling him. His companions spilled to a halt about them, peering at Longarm from under the rims of their hats, their faces hard, questioning. Still more riders came up, lifting out of the tall grass with barely a sound.

"Name's Long," Longarm said to the lead rider.

"Tom Goodnight," the fellow replied, holding out his hand.

Longarm shook it. The grip was powerful. Goodnight rode tall in the saddle, a bony, loose-jointed fellow with a lantern jaw and a powerful hook of a nose. His eyes were dark and smoky, an Indian's eyes.

"Ellen Buckman sends her best wishes."

The man's face softened immediately. "She sent you?"

Longarm nodded. "There's a batch of hostiles on my tail, so she gave me directions to your place."

"I see them. Who are they?"

"Matt Forman and his crew."

One of Goodnight's riders had pulled up on a slight rise beyond them and was looking north. He called out to Goodnight, telling him that the Lazy M riders were coming fast and hard. Goodnight smiled, his teeth a white slash in his tanned face.

"Good," he said, looking around at his men. "See to your weapons and stand fast," he told them.

As his men checked the loads in their revolvers and levered fresh cartridges into their Winchesters, Goodnight asked Longarm, "Why are they after you, Long, if you don't mind my asking."

"I want Matt Forman's brother, Gil."

"This a private score you have with that rattlesnake?"

"Yes and no. I'm a lawman, but I don't have a warrant. Gil Forman's out of my jurisdiction. I'm a deputy U.S. marshal from Denver."

"You've come a long way, mister."

"Like from another country."

"That's about the size of it."

Goodnight looked around at his men. Their guns were out and gleaming in the morning light. Their horses, which seemed to have caught the scent of the approaching riders and the tension they brought with them, were acting up some.

"Dismount and spread out," Goodnight told his men. "Keep low in the grass." He glanced over at Longarm. "Stick by me, Long, in case hot lead starts flying."

"I don't want it to come to that."

"I do."

Goodnight's men dismounted and pulled back behind the grassy ridges and swales surrounding this low spot and promptly vanished, as completely and as efficiently as ghosts. For an instant Longarm heard the soft thud of their horses' hooves on the heavy grass, and then nothing.

Goodnight and Longarm rode up onto a grassy knoll and pulled to a halt. For some time the Lazy M riders were out of sight as they traversed a long gully. When they popped up again they were much closer, and Longarm was able to make out Matt and Gil Forman well out in front of the others. As soon as they saw Goodnight

50

and Longarm, they reined in, upraised arms signaling a halt to the men strung out behind them.

As their riders caught up to them, Longarm counted eight men in all. After a quick conference with their riders, Matt and Gil Forman broke from them and rode toward Longarm and Goodnight. When they were close enough to make themselves heard, they pulled to a halt, their riders fanning out behind them in a ragged line, each man sitting his mount alertly, expectantly.

"What is this, Goodnight?" Matt demanded. "How come you're sidin' with this here lawman?"

"You didn't think I'd take *your* side, did you?"

"Maybe you don't understand, Tom. That son of a bitch beside you is fixin' to take my brother to a hanging."

"Yes. So I understand."

"And you're still siding him?"

"You know what, Matt? I was disappointed when I heard Long was only interested in Gil."

"What's that?"

"Something wrong with your hearin'? What I'm wishin' is he could take you in when he takes Gil. Take away some of the stink hangin' over them hills back of you. Do the air good. Freshen it up, it would."

The insult was studied and ferocious, and its barb sank deep. Longarm saw Matt flinch with fury. Beside him, Gil leaned forward over his cantle like a cur straining on a leash.

"What're we sitting here for? We can take them!" Gil snarled. "There's only the two of them!"

Goodnight unholstered his Colt and sent a quick round into the air. Before the echo of the detonation faded, there came the soft, rapid drumming of horses' hooves on the thick grass as Goodnight's men swept up out of the gullies and swales surrounding them and closed in, their ready Winchesters resting across their pommels.

Glancing quickly about him at the enclosing circle of riders, Matt snarled, "You son of a bitch, Goodnight! You tricked us!"

"Damn your eyes!" panted Gil.

Goodnight smiled coldly. "Tell you what I'll do, gents. I'll send another shot over your heads. If you're not on your way by then, I'll just lower this here revolver and keep on firing."

"You ain't heard the last of this!" Matt cried.

"I sincerely hope not."

Goodnight fired a second shot. The round seared the air over Matt Forman's head, close enough for him to hear it. Matt flung his horse around, Gil following, and the two raced back through the ranks of their own men, who spun their horses in turn and followed swiftly after them.

Longarm and Tom Goodnight were relaxing on Tom's porch, seated in homemade wooden chairs covered with buffalo robes. Longarm had lit a cheroot and Tom was enjoying his pipe. A brown jug sat between them on the porch's planks. Twice already Longarm had sampled its contents, and while it was definitely not Maryland rye, the fiery applejack had enough of a wallop to serve the purpose for which it was intended.

Longarm had just finished telling Goodnight why he wanted to bring Gil Forman back to Denver. His brows knitted in thought, Goodnight got up abruptly and began pacing.

"Seems to me, Long, you aren't going to have any luck bringing that man in. His brother will see to that. And without a warrant, you really have no legal rights in the matter. Even if you did manage to subdue Gil Forman and bring him in, it would be tantamount to kidnapping. Maybe you better pull back some and decide which side of the law you're on."

"There's truth in what you say, Tom," Longarm admitted ruefully. "The thing is, I came here thinking Seth Barton was undercover, and that together we could pick up Gil and take him back with a minimum of fuss."

"There's little chance of that now."

"I know. The cat's out of the bag. But I'm not going to back off. I can't do that."

"I can understand how you feel." Goodnight stopped pacing and looked shrewdly at Longarm. "On the other hand, if you were to catch that little son of a bitch in the act of rustling cattle, wouldn't that change matters, at least enough for you to take some kind of action against him?"

Longarm looked shrewdly at Tom. He knew at once what the man was thinking. "You mean rustling your cattle, Tom?"

"That's what I mean."

"You're talking about the Big Burnout, aren't you."

"You know about that place?"

"Yes. What have you got in mind?"

"Three days ago I heard—from a friendly hill rancher —that there might be an attempt to rustle some of the stock I'm grazing on the north forty. As usual, the cattle would be driven to the burnout, and that would be the end of it. So I sent two of my best riders out there to watch."

"To watch?"

"Yes. Just to watch. And then to trail any riders who drove off any of my stock, if necessary, right into the burnout. See where the hell it is in there they keep the cattle."

"For how long now have your men been watching the herd?"

"Since yesterday."

"It couldn't be the Lazy M then. Gil and Matt Forman and his crew have been hard on my tail during that time. And you just sent them hightailing out of here."

"But not all his men, Longarm. I noticed right off that Clem Jagger, Matt's foreman, was missing from that bunch tailing you, along with ten of their meanest riders." Goodnight gazed moodily to the northwest. "What that means to me is that Clem Jagger and his riders had business elsewhere. Clem and those ten riders would be more than sufficient to drive off my herd."

"How much longer are you going to wait for your men to return?"

"Not too much longer."

"Maybe we should take a ride tomorrow morning, then. First thing."

Goodnight nodded grimly. "If they don't get back before then."

"You worried?"

"Sure, I'm worried." Goodnight looked closely at Longarm. "By the way, do you mind telling me how you knew about the burnout?"

"Kate Summerfield told me."

"Ah, yes. Kate. She's the one that has Matt Forman by the tail—and can't let go."

"She might be getting ready to do just that," Longarm said. "What I can't understand is how she could have got mixed up with Matt Forman in the first place."

"That's simple. She's convinced herself there's nothing wrong with Matt. His brother Gil is the problem. She blames Gil for everything."

"I caught that. She doesn't like Gil much at all."

"For all Kate's strength and wisdom, in this one thing she is a fool. Gil Forman is the creation of his brother Matt. He brought Gil up. Every mean trick, every foul blow, every curse that drops from his lips is the result of Matt's tutelage. They are two sides of the same coin."

"This warning you got, about the rustling, I mean. Was it Ellen's father that sent it to you?"

"Yes. Through Ellen."

"She's a fine woman," Longarm said.

"I know. As soon as this trouble with the Lazy M gets cleared away, I'm going to marry that woman."

"What about her old man?"

"I can handle him."

"Good luck."

"Thanks." He slumped back down in his chair and hooked the jug up onto his shoulder. After pouring the applejack down his throat, he wiped his mouth off with the back of his hand and passed it to Longarm. "When we ride out tomorrow to look for those two riders of mine, will you be coming along?"

"Wouldn't miss it for the world."

Goodnight's long face cracked into a pleased smile. "Glad to have you aboard, Longarm."

• • •

The bunkhouse door swung open. Goodnight's tall frame filled it. Longarm sat up in his bunk and watched as a match flared in Goodnight's hand and he lit a lantern hanging on the wall beside the door.

"Riders coming!" Goodnight called out to his men. "Comin' hard. I don't like the sound of it."

Longarm pulled on his britches and reached for his .44 resting in the holster hanging from a nail over his bunk. On bare feet he padded to the doorway and stood beside Goodnight. The growing mutter of distant hooves came from the northwest.

Goodnight's crew poured out past him and took positions in the darkness, flanking the bunkhouse and the main house. Dark riders spilled out of the night, gunfire erupting from their midst. A bunkhouse window splintered. More rounds slammed into the side of the bunkhouse and then the lantern went. Goodnight ducked back inside to smother the flaming shards of glass that lay on the floor, then hurried back out, he and Longarm clambering up onto the porch for a clearer view of the night riders.

They kept on charging across the yard, their gun flashes illuminating their faces too briefly for Longarm to be able to make out any of them. Longarm found himself firing almost without willing it, his Colt thundering in his hand like a thing alive, the smell of cordite strong in his nostrils.

By the time the riders had swept across the yard, he had reloaded twice and was still firing steadily into their plunging mass when they turned in a body, swept alongside the long porch fronting the main house, and sent a withering fire into it. Longarm felt the porch under his feet splintering and heard the hot passage of lead as it slammed past him and into the log walls. The riders took out all but one window, then swerved away and galloped back the way they had come, keeping low in the saddle, no longer firing. In a moment they had swept out of the yard and vanished into the night.

"Hold your fire!" Goodnight cried.

As the firing ceased, Longarm leaned back against the side of the house, aware that he was holding an empty, smoking revolver. He glanced over at Goodnight and saw a thin trickle of blood moving down his cheek.

"You hit?" Longarm asked.

"Just a nick." Goodnight chuckled nervously. "I was lucky. The round struck me in the head. Nothing to worry about." He walked to the edge of the porch and peered about him into the darkness. "Anybody take a hit?"

"Pete stopped one," one of his men called up to him.

"It's nothing, boss," cried Pete. "It's just a flesh wound."

"Have it looked at," Goodnight told him.

Goodnight's foreman, Sam Dunstan, stepped up onto the porch. He was wearing only the bottoms of his long johns and had two smoking Colts in his hands. "Now what the hell was that all about?"

Like most of them, he was gazing in the direction the riders had taken. The pound of hoofbeats had ceased entirely, and the crickets and fireflies had taken back the night. From all about them in the darkness came the relieved cursing and muttering of the men as they straightened out of their crouches or left whatever cover they had found, their tone revealing the relief they felt at not having stopped any of the lead that had been pouring in on them.

"I don't like it," Goodnight told Longarm, his voice low. "This ain't the end of it, I'm thinking."

"Seems like they came to deliver something."

"My thoughts exactly."

Goodnight was telling his foreman to look around to make sure no one besides Pete was hurt, when one of his men standing over by the horse barn cried out, his voice close to panic.

"What is it?" Goodnight demanded, jumping off the porch and striding swiftly toward him.

"It's Biff and Willy! They're hurt bad. Them riders must've dumped them."

Longarm followed Goodnight, then stood back as the owner of the Circle T and his foreman bent over the two men. Longarm did not have to be told that these were the two riders Goodnight had sent to watch over the northern herd.

They had been caught trailing the rustlers, obviously. One man was twisting slowly on the ground, like a huge worm someone had stomped on. He was so fearfully torn up it was difficult for Longarm to believe the man was still alive. His companion was trying to sit up, his eyes staring blindly about him, his head and shoulders a bloody, ribboned mess. It was clear both men had been dragged most of the way back to the Circle T, for still bound around their ankles were lengths of rope, the trailing ends of which had been neatly cut through. It was their heads and shoulders that had taken the worst punishment.

"Biff," Goodnight said softly to the one trying to sit up, "who did this to you?"

Biff's voice came in a hoarse, barely audible whisper. "Clem Jagger."

"What happened?"

"Will and I . . . we saw them. They cut out most of the herd and drove it to the burnout. We did like you said, boss . . . we went in after them to see which way they went . . . but they was waitin' for us." His head sagged and he began to cough, a harsh racking sound, and Longarm saw the man was coughing up blood. "They must've seen us tailin' 'em."

"You'll swear to this, Biff? It was Clem Jagger? He's the one did this to you?"

Biff nodded weakly. "It was him, all right."

Goodnight stood up and told Dunstan to hitch up the buckboard, that both men were going to have to be taken in to Doc Wolfson in Placer Town that night. Then he asked for and got volunteers to ride shotgun. This was a range war now, he told his men grimly, and no Circle T rider was to go anywhere alone or unarmed.

Later, while Longarm was sipping hot coffee in the cookshack with Goodnight, discussing what their next move ought to be, the foreman entered, hat in hand, his face white, and told Goodnight it would not be necessary to take the wounded men into Placer Town.

Both men were dead.

Chapter 5

A preacher came out of the hills sometime before noon on an old gray horse, conducted the funeral for the two men, took his dinner, and went away. Later that same day, just before dusk, Longarm thanked Goodnight for his hospitality and rode back through the pass. He was leaving Goodnight free to deal with the Lazy M in whatever way he chose, without a lawman—however far from his jurisdiction and however sympathetic—looking over his shoulder. As for himself, it was Gil Forman he wanted before he got caught up in a range war.

He was at least five miles into the timber beyond the pass, moving through growing darkness, when he heard the first faint pound of another rider in the night, coming up on him from behind. He turned off the trail he was following and pulled up behind a clump of aspen. But as he sat his horse to wait for the rider to pass him, the horseman's steady beat faded, heading off south, in the direction of Placer Town—or the road leading to Ellen Buckman's Sun Ranch.

Longarm swung back down onto the trail, crossed it and followed the lone horseman's dying echo into the trees. Keeping a steady pace through the dim files of timber was not easy. The sky above, though brilliantly awash with stars, shed only the faintest patina of light onto the overhanging branches and the uncertain trail ahead of him. A cooling wind flowed downhill, its faint, fragrant pressure beating gently upon him.

Close to two hours later he felt the horse growing slack under him and decided he had better stop to give it a rest. He was looking for a stream to make camp when he heard the sullen pound of many hooves coming from a road or trail in the timber below him. Whoever they were, they were pushing their mounts hard. Pulling up, he lifted his head to listen as the dim thunder of hooves increased, reached a peak not more than three hundred yards beyond him, then fell off rapidly to the south.

Starting up again, he followed the fading sound as rapidly as he could. The horse frequently slowed under him, shaking its head occasionally in protest. It knew its own mind and was anxious for that rest it had sensed coming earlier. But Longarm urged it on without stint, an alarm growing deep within him as he reached, then passed south of, the lone, blackened pine Ellen had pointed out to him earlier.

A moment later came the first rattle of gunfire, the faint popping sound borne on the cool night wind. It came from the Sun Ranch. He knew that almost for a certainty as he broke into the notch of the sloping, timbered canyon above it. Its high walls held him to the trail's almost-eccentric windings and cutbacks as he followed it to the ranch. He urged the flagging horse to a faster pace. The firing was constant now, not heavy volleys, but at a steady, brisk pace, the way it would sound if dug-in forces were sending lead at a target.

At last he broke out onto the timbered slope above the ranch. Charging his horse on down through it, he crossed the meadow and the road and continued on up the gentle slope to the ranch buildings. Approaching the rear of the big horse barn, he snatched his rifle from its scabbard and leapt from his spent horse. As the animal pulled up and trotted gratefully away into the night, Longarm scaled the corral fence and ran the remaining distance to the rear of the barn, entering through the back door.

He heard someone in the front of the barn at one of the windows firing a Colt steadily. The man was making such a racket and enjoying himself so hugely, he did not hear Longarm come up behind him. A powerful stench of raw whiskey clung to him like a curse. Longarm used the barrel of his Colt to club the man to the floor. When he stirred sluggishly and tried to regain his feet, Longarm kicked him in the face, sending him reeling senseless into a nearby stall.

Peering out through the window, Longarm saw a column of thick, black smoke just beginning to pulse from the ranch house's rear window. A second later, the rear of the house exploded in flames. The front was still untouched by the fire, and from one of its windows came a desultory, useless fire. Crouching figures posted all about the yard were busy pouring a steady volley into the ranch house. In an effort to bully completely any who might still be alive inside the burning building, the attackers were apparently content simply to blaze away at what windows still remained intact.

Levering his Winchester, Longarm picked out one shadowy figure close to a corner of the porch, and aiming just behind the flash of his six-gun, squeezed off a shot. The man cried out and pitched forward into the darkness, his gun suddenly silent. Levering swiftly, Longarm fired on two more attackers, and at once found himself a target. With slugs whining in past the shattered window and punching through the barn's thin walls, Longarm clambered up into the loft, and from the hay loading window continued to pour fire down on the shadowy figures scuttling frantically about below him, his Winchester growing warm with its steady employment.

By now the flames were sending a garish pretence of daylight over the yard, giving the attackers less and less concealment. Abruptly someone to the right of the barn shouted to his men, telling them to pull out. It was Matt Forman; Longarm recognized his harsh voice immediately. Lugging their wounded men with them, the attackers bolted from the yard to their horses beyond the corral. In a moment they had mounted up and galloped off. Before they vanished into the night, Longarm managed to get a quick glimpse of Matt Forman, but saw no sign of his brother Gil.

Longarm dropped to the ground and raced up the porch and into the burning ranch house. It felt as if he had charged into the open door of a furnace, which in truth he had. Shrouded in low, choking coils of smoke just ahead of him, Ellen was dragging her father's limp body out of the kitchen. Longarm brushed past her, lifted the injured man in his arms, and hurried out onto the porch, herding Ellen ahead of him.

In the yard beyond the porch, she turned to look up at him, her eyes wild with concern. "Abe!" she cried. "He's still in there. He's been hit!"

Longarm put her father down inside the barn, left them, and darted back into the inferno. Peering through the smoke, he was just able to make out Abe's slumped figure alongside a shattered window. His eyes smarting fiercely, he rushed through the smoke, slung Abe over his shoulder, and ducked out of the house. As he stumbled down the porch steps with his burden, he was coughing and his eyes were streaming so, he had to keep blinking in order to see where he was going.

Shielded behind the barn door from the searing heat, Ellen was crouched down beside her father. As Longarm lowered Abe gently to the barn floor beside Buckman, he glanced at Ellen's father and saw that the man's eyes were open, and in the reflected light cast by the fire he saw a grim, angry determination to stay alive.

Turning his attention back to Abe, Longarm looked more closely at a ragged hole in the old man's chest. Resting the back of his hand against Abe's neck artery, Longarm found no pulse. He closed Abe's lids and threw a saddle blanket over him, then turned to Ellen.

She looked up at him through tears. "Dead?"

Longarm nodded. "I know it was Matt Forman and the Lazy M," he told her. "But why?"

Buckman spoke up, his voice soft but distinct.

"Matt's gone crazy. He wants to drive them cattlemen on the other side of the range off their land. He don't care how he does it. And he's bringin' in the rest of the hill ranchers, making them join up with him."

"Dad tried to stop them," Ellen said, "to get them to stand up to Matt."

"And this is how Matt stops him."

"Yes," she said, tears rolling down her cheeks.

Longarm chucked his hat back off his head and looked quickly around, a sudden frown on his face. "Where's the rest of your crew?"

"One of the men rode in and warned the crew what was up. They lit out. Abe was the only one who stayed." She glanced over at his dead body. "I wish now he hadn't."

Longarm bent close to examine Ellen's father. The man was lying on his back now, his eyes closed, his breathing labored, an unpleasant wheezing sound coming from him. He had been wounded in his chest, but the round had entered above his lungs, and Longarm was hoping nothing vital had been hit. But he didn't like the way it sounded and realized the wound might very well prove fatal if Buckman did not get to a doctor, and soon.

"You better get your father into Placer Town," he told Ellen, "so Doc Wolfson can take a look at him."

"That quack?"

"He's all you got."

She glanced around at the body of the man Longarm had sent reeling into the stall. "What are we going to do about that man over there?"

"Never mind him."

Longarm stepped over to the open barn door and peered across the yard at the still-blazing ranch house. Its roof had already collapsed, and it looked as if the only thing that would remain upright would be the fireplace and chimney. Ellen appeared in the doorway beside him. Longarm glanced at her. Tears rolled without shame down her cheeks as she watched the destruction of what had been her home.

"Come on," Longarm said, having no words to comfort the woman. "I'll help you hitch up that team."

Ellen followed Longarm back into the barn.

With the first light of dawn, Ellen left with her father.

Longarm watched the flatbed wagon disappear down the road, then walked into the barn and turned his attention to the gunman still lying unconscious in the horse stall. Longarm nudged him until the man stirred, then stepped back to watch the man sit up groggily, both hands holding his aching head. There was a gash on the side of his chin where Longarm's boot had struck it. He still stank of whiskey, and Longarm figured it was this as much as his boot that had kept him on ice this long.

None too gently, Longarm hauled the man upright. "I want some information."

"Who the hell're you?"

"You should show me more respect. I'm the one that kicked you in the head. That was Matt Forman leading your bunch last night, wasn't it?"

"Sure."

"Where's Gil?"

"How the hell do I know?"

"I think you better tell me."

66

The man moistened dry lips and tried to pull free of Longarm's grasp. "What's in it for me if I tell you?"

"That's easy. I won't rub your nose in horse shit."

For a moment or two the man looked closely at Longarm, as if measuring Longarm's tenacity. Then he shrugged. "Gil rode out."

"That's no help," Longarm told him grimly, grabbing the man about his collar.

Gasping, the man blurted out, "North! He rode north!"

"That's not good enough," Longarm told him, his fingers tightening.

"All right! All right!" the Lazy M rider cried, clawing frantically at Longarm's steel-cable fingers. "He's headin' for Silver Creek. I heard him and his brother talkin'. You're pushin' Gil too hard. He might go over the border."

Longarm let go. The Lazy M puncher flung himself back, coming up hard against the edge of the stall. With both hands up to his neck, he sucked in great gutfuls of air.

"Get on your horse and clear out," Longarm told him. "And keep riding."

A moment later Longarm watched the Lazy M gunslick ride out, heading south. Longarm had no confidence the man would continue in that direction, but that hardly mattered, in any case. He went for his horse, his brow knit in thought.

Why in hell would Gil Forman be fleeing to Canada? With his brother Matt at his side, he should have considered himself safe enough in these hills. Hell, damn near invulnerable.

Perhaps Matt had heard about the evidence Longarm

carried in his saddlebag and had sent him packing. Perhaps. It was a possibility that did not entirely convince Longarm, especially now that he had gotten to know Matt Forman. He thought then of another possibility: Gil was on Lazy M business, maybe driving Goodnight's stolen herd to Silver Creek to sell it.

Now, that made sense. Gil Forman was combining business with discretion.

Longarm rode north once more, cutting toward a high pass that reared in the distance. As he rode he could not help reflecting that in the few short days since he had arrived in this country, he had found himself astride a wave of violence and death that, from all appearances, had yet to crest.

This grim awareness hung over him like a cloud as he rode, despite the day's bright sunshine. When at last he found himself at the point of the vaulting range where it tilted up into sheer rock faces, he paused to look back the way he had come—at the timbered hills and valleys, the meadows and flats scattered between them like torn scraps of clothing—and wondered if any land, especially these dark, gnarled hills, could be worth the bloodshed and anguish they brought with them.

He turned about in his saddle and peered up through the sparse timber at the rocky slope before him, and with a fatalistic shrug, nudged his horse on up through the sparse timber. Before long he found himself following a faint trail around boulders and steep cliff faces that took him close by white fields of snow. Occasional warped and stunted conifers found a hold in the rocks' narrow cracks. A hardy grass Longarm had never seen before battled with them for the little soil that remained. Sharp winds raced along every canyon and swept Longarm with the clean cold of the stars. By noon he was lost in this profound upland labyrinth of rock and great slashed canyons that twisted and fell, and tumbled and angled and doubled back. For a while it looked as if he would not be able to escape the ring of penning peaks.

And then he found something to guide him, a cattle trail. Daily rains had beaten upon it and the cattle's hooves had pulverized the soft rock into a pale, unmistakable trail. As it narrowed, Longarm noticed where the cattle had been hazed through the tight defiles, leaving tufts of hair wedged into cracks in the walls. In his mind's eye he could see the steers milling frantically as they were pushed along, the air filled with dust and the sound of ropes smacking hides.

Once, where the shale-littered trail threaded the edge of a deep canyon, Longarm saw far below him the carcass of a steer. Dismounting, he climbed down to the bottom of the dank canyon. It was narrow, and a tiny stream of snow water had cut its floor. The steer lay across the stream, a little bloated. On the left hip, which was uppermost, Longarm saw that a generous patch of the hide had been cut out, the brand along with it.

Climbing back up to his horse, he continued on, and by midafternoon came to a tight, flat valley that widened out between sheer cliffs. There was no grass in it, but there was a stream that raced its course against one wall. He circled the flat and found the remains of a recent campfire, built on the dead, blackened core of countless other campfires. He rode on into more canyon country, and when night came, picked a sheltered spot off the trail and camped there. He had no food for himself and no grain for his horse. He unsaddled it, rubbed it down, then rolled up in his slicker under a shelf of rock.

He was surprised the next morning at how well he had slept. And at how ravenous he was. By daylight he was on the trail again, a raw wind that smelled of rain beating in his face. It seemed to him as he traveled between these rugged, cold peaks that this range was endless, and that all he would ever see again would be mountain peaks shrouded in thunderheads. But by mid-afternoon he found himself leaning in his saddle and realized he was traveling downslope. Soon, poking through the gray mists below him, he saw the tops of thin pines. Before long he was once again riding through green, fragrant timber, free at last of the cold mountain walls.

At first he could see only a widening gap in the cloud-shrouded mountains, but as he rode on, he glimpsed through the trees below him a dark, wide valley folded in between the peaks. It was green enough, but it was the cold green of pines and junipers ready to receive rain. He kept on, still following the dim cattle trail, until he reached the valley floor, where the trail merged with other trails and soon became lost among them.

He had made it over the northern reaches of the range, and the trail he had followed had told him much. On the valley floor, he came onto a rutted road and was soon having to make way for the huge ore wagons with their six- and eight- and ten-horse teams pulling them.

His direction sent him further into the valley and he soon found himself moving along a wide, rapid stream. Glancing up at the mountain flanks on either side, he could barely make out the mist-shrouded mine shacks clinging to their steep sides.

Not one of the crew on the huge ore wagons that rumbled past paid the slightest attention to him, and he took this to mean that riders from the other side of the range were no strangers to this land. He kept on, and where the valley narrowed, he found Silver Creek, a rough, unpainted settlement of raw buildings and board shacks fronting a wide street fetlock-deep in mud. The place was, above all, busy. The heavy ore wagons had churned the streets into barely navigable swamps, the mud holes axle-deep in spots. The drivers of the ore wagons uttered fierce and terrible imprecations at those foolish enough to drive buckboards and other frail rigs before them. Meanwhile, the early-morning mist had dissolved into a steady, miserable rain, while the men and the few women thronging the board sidewalks did their best to ignore it.

Longarm worked his way down the jammed street to the livery stable, where he gave his tired horse over to a boy for graining. Leaving his gear above the stall he had rented, he left the livery and joined the crowd moving along the narrow boardwalks. The townspeople were a motley, unforgiving lot. Longarm noted among them mule skinners, prospectors, gamblers, promoters of all sorts, and overall, an unusual preponderance of cold-eyed gunslicks, their hips agleam with well-oiled six-guns.

Pausing under a general store's wooden awning,

Longarm looked about to get his bearings. The steady din around him was familiar enough, but Longarm did not like the feel of the town. It made him edgy. Silver Creek was an unholy mix. It was both a mining and a border town, a perfect place to draw the get-rich-quick schemers on the one hand, the desperadoes and gun-slicks on the other. A perfect place to bring rustled cattle.

Longarm caught sight of what appeared to be the biggest and gaudiest saloon in town. It was called The Bonanza. He left the awning's protection and walked through the rain to the saloon, mounted the steps, and shouldered his way through the bat-wings. It was still early in the afternoon, but the place was crowded, the air vibrant with the loud, steady hum of men's voices raised occasionally to a shout or a yip, the clink of poker chips, and the rattle of tumbling dice.

The bar was along the right wall, an ornate, heavy affair of thick, highly polished mahogany, a magnificent, bar-length mirror behind it. The rest of the big place was shabby in comparison. With some amusement Longarm noted that the glasses had been stacked before the mirror so as to hide three jagged cracks that had been busted into it.

As he pushed to the bar, he looked around. All the gambling tables—poker, monte, faro—were doing a brisk business. Reaching the bar, he ordered Maryland rye from the barkeep. Without so much as a cocked eyebrow, the round-cheeked, cheerful fellow produced a bottle of the desired brand and a fresh, clean glass to go with it.

As Longarm poured, he said, "A man might have left

word for me here. He'd be bringin' in a herd. He told me to meet him here."

"Who're you?"

"Long. Custis Long."

"Where you from?"

Longarm smiled. "You wouldn't know the place. A little town in Oregon, near the coast. Any word?"

The barkeep, as Longarm had hoped he would, consulted with the other three bartenders, who looked toward Longarm and shook their heads negatively. Unsatisfied, the barkeep called for the swamper, who was soon passing among the percentage girls, asking the same question.

Longarm waited, the rye warming him, helping slightly to ward off the close, fetid smell of unwashed men and wet feet coming at him from all directions. At the far end of the bar, the saloon opened up into a larger room, where most of the percentage girls were seated at tables with their men. From there, steps led upstairs to a balcony, where the girls' had their cribs. As Longarm watched, he saw girls moving up the stairs with their customers, some with their arms draped over their shoulders, others with their hands poked down past the men's belt buckles.

He turned his head idly to watch the piano player on a raised platform flailing away at his upright. The piano was dismally out of tune, but in the general tumult and hubbub no one seemed to notice, or care.

A voice behind him said, "You Long?"

He turned to find one of the bar girls facing him. She was dark, with a lovely face as hard as marble, and curious, surface-lighted black eyes. Her dress was black, cheap, clinging, full of her ripe, voluptuous body as she leaned against the bar.

"Yes," Longarm said.

"Buy me a drink and we can take a table in back."

Longarm ordered a drink for her and followed her into the bar's larger section under the balcony. They took a table in the corner, and when her drink came she sipped it sparingly, while he stayed with his rye. Her drink was mostly water, Longarm realized.

Putting her drink down, she tipped her head mischievously. "You a cattle buyer?"

Longarm nodded. "Sure. Do you own any?"

"Someone I know does."

"He got a name?"

She was studying Longarm with frank, observing eyes, and finally she said quietly, "I think you know it already. Gil Forman."

"I think maybe I do. Where is he?"

"Upstairs with a gun trained on both of us. You're supposed to go up there with me."

There was something in her voice and in her glance that warmed him, despite the circumstances. "I'll bet you weren't supposed to tell me that part—about the gun, I mean."

She smiled. "You're right. I wasn't."

"Why did you?"

"I'm a fool."

"That the only reason?"

She tossed her hair defiantly, her dark eyes exploding with malice. "I hate that son of a bitch, Gil Forman, and his brother, too. Maybe I hate his brother more."

74

He poured himself another shot of the rye. "What's your name?"

"Teresa. Tionetta is my real name. I am Italian, but they want me to be Spanish, so I am."

"What shall I call you?"

She shrugged. "Call me Teresa. I will answer to it."

"Is Gil alone up there?"

"His foreman is with him. A man called Clem Jagger."

"I don't think I ever met the man. What's he look like?"

"Jagger? He is all bull, that man. He has big shoulders and a big belly and his eyes are too close together."

"That's the only one with Gil?"

"He has already sold his herd. The men who came with him have returned to his ranch. I think Gil was going on to Canada. But I think now he's hoping to kill you, so he can stay in Montana."

"And that's why he wants you to bring me upstairs?"

"Yes. You are such a fool to walk in here like you just did. I feel sorry for you."

"He saw me from the balcony, did he?"

"He was with me. One of the girls told him a buyer from Oregon named Long was looking for cattle. He left my room and saw you, then told me to come down here and bring you up to him."

"How much time did he give you?"

She shrugged. "Not much. I think you better finish your drink."

"And go up there with you?"

"He said he will kill me if I don't get you to come up with me."

Longarm finished his drink and stopped the bottle. His creaky ruse had worked well enough. He knew precisely where Gil Forman was. His only problem now was to collar the son of a bitch without endangering Teresa. He glanced at her covertly.

"Tell me where he is right now. Precisely."

"Behind you. Almost directly overhead."

"His gun is unholstered?"

"Yes, at his side."

Longarm glanced around. The saloon was as noisy as ever, the faro table busy, the clink of poker chips in the air, the piano still tinkling out of tune. But all three barkeeps were keeping a wary eye on him, he realized, and Longarm saw one of them glance nervously up at the balcony.

"I can't do anything sudden," Longarm told Teresa, "or he'll know you tipped me."

"Be careful. I don't want your blood on my hands."

"I think it's time we went upstairs." Longarm got to his feet. "Act casual. Take my arm and lean on it as you steer me toward the stairway."

She got up and thrust her hand through the crook of his arm. He lifted his bottle of rye from the table and they headed for the stairway. Teresa played her part well, leaning her head against his shoulder as they mounted the stairs, while he apparently kept his attention focused entirely on her.

When they reached the balcony, Teresa guided his steps toward her room, chatting softly with him, only her eyes revealing the tension she felt. Longarm saw no sign of Gil, but that did not surprise him. Teresa stopped at her door and reached for the knob. Before she could turn it, the door swung open and Longarm saw a grinning Gil Forman standing in the doorway, a drawn revolver in his hand. Beside him stood Clem Jagger, matching Teresa's description perfectly.

As if he were furious with Teresa for tricking him, Longarm swore and flung the girl to one side. As she stumbled away from him, Gil looked past Longarm. "You did fine, bitch," he told her. "Not get your hot ass downstairs and keep your mouth shut."

Longarm heard her hurried flight down the stairs, noticing at the same time a sudden hush from the saloon below. He looked Jagger over with some interest. After all, this was the same worthy who had been forced to flee for his life when Kate Summerfield sent a blast of buckshot through her kitchen window.

Gil Forman, meanwhile, was enjoying himself hugely. He turned to smile at Jagger, his yellow teeth gleaming in his grimy, unshaven face.

"Look what we got here, Clem. A big man. Come all the way from Denver to take me in."

"Maybe we better turn tail and run."

Covering Longarm carefully, Gil stepped close, reached in under Longarm's jacket, and withdrew the .44 from his cross-draw holster. Then Gil stepped back through the doorway and waggled his gun.

"Get in here, Long."

Longarm walked in past the two men. Teresa's crib was little more than a long closet with a single window looking out over the back alley. There was barely enough room in it for the girl's cot. As Jagger closed the door, Longarm saw Gil reaching down for a pillow to muffle the crack of his revolver.

While mounting the stairs, Longarm had shoved the whiskey bottle down between the small of his back and his waistband. Now he reached back for it, and with all the force he could muster in the cramped room, swung the bottle around, shattering it on the side of Gil's head. Gil pitched forward across the cot, his head crunching into the wall with numbing force.

Turning his attention to Jagger, Longarm grabbed the foreman about the shirt collar with both hands, and with all his force ran the man past him and out through the window. The heavyset man went through it head down, shoulder first, glass and window sash flying. Poking his head out through the shattered window, Longarm peered down. It was still raining, the rutted back alley gleaming with puddles. Jagger had landed on his back, and as Longarm watched, the big foreman rolled over once, splashed through a puddle, then collapsed facedown in the muck.

Longarm left the window and hurried over to Gil Forman, who was twisting slowly on the cot, groaning. Longarm took back from him his .44 and then disarmed Forman. Rolling him over, he aroused him by slapping him hard on both cheeks a couple of times. As soon as Gil was sitting up, Longarm thrust his .44's long barrel under his chin, lifted the man off the cot, and nudged him toward the door. Longarm opened it for him, stepped back, and guided him on through the doorway and out onto the balcony, the pressure from the gun barrel causing Gil to rise up onto his tiptoes. As they started down the hallway, they met a large, noisy crowd swarming up the stairs and then along the balcony toward them.

Two men were leading the pack.

At first glance they appeared to be cattlemen, the older and shorter one a middle-aged man in black trousers, half boots and Stetson, pearl-handled six-guns slung low on each hip. The other one was younger, swarthy, and wore a slicker shiny with rain.

"What're you doin' with Gil there, mister?" the older man asked.

"Who are you?"

"I'm the town marshal. Brothers is the name. This here's my deputy, Colson."

"My name's Long," Longarm told them. "I'm a deputy U.S. marshal. I'm on official business."

"You know anything about that man just landed in the alley?"

"He came after me. Tried to prevent me from arresting Gil."

Brothers chuckled. "Then it was you sent him out through that window?"

"I told you. I had no choice."

"Don't listen to him, Charlie!" Gil told him, his head twisted unnaturally away from the muzzle of Longarm's gun. "He ain't got no warrant! This here's a frame-up!"

Brothers stepped closer. "Maybe you'd like to show me your warrant, Long."

"I don't have one, Brothers."

His face got very pleasant, his smile easy. "Well, then, maybe you'd better put that iron away and let Gil go."

"He's a murderer."

"Them's strong words, Long."

"If I let Forman go, he'll take off for Canada."

"Relax, Long. Gil won't do that." He smiled blandly at Gil. "You'll stay in town if I ask you, won't you, Gil?"

"Sure, Charlie," Gil replied eagerly, a grin breaking across his face. "You have my word."

"There you are, Long. You have Gil's word."

"Get out of my way, Brothers. You're obstructing justice."

Brothers, his face still amiable, let his hands drop to the butts of his pearl-handled revolvers. "Looks to me like you're the one obstructing justice, tryin' to arrest a man without a warrant. Now, if you want, Long, we can make this real unpleasant for you. But you bein' a fellow law officer an' all, I don't suppose you'd want to do anything that foolish. You heard Gil. He's given his word."

As Brothers spoke, his deputy, Colson, shifted slightly to one side, his eyes cold, one hand dropping to the butt of his six-gun. Longarm was facing not one but two gunslicks, he realized, both perfectly willing to end matters right there, if that was what it took. He let his .44 drop. Swiftly Gil ducked away from him and burst through the onlookers crowding the balcony. It did not take him long to disappear down the stairs.

Brothers stepped forward and took the gun out of Longarm's hand and stuck it into his belt. Then he stepped back. "Okay, Long. Let's take a trip to my office, so you can let me know what this is all about."

Seething inwardly, Longarm allowed the two lawmen to escort him out of the saloon and down the street through the thinning rain to the town marshal's office. Once inside it, Brothers slumped into his chair, pulled out a drawer, and leaned back, resting a boot on the edge of the open drawer.

"Now what's all this about, Long?" he asked, as he lifted a bottle of whiskey out of a drawer.

"Never mind. It wouldn't do any good for me to tell you," Longarm told him. "You're not interested in seeing Gil Forman answer for a murder."

"Murder, you say?"

"Yes."

"Who? Some drunk tried to draw on him? You can't blame a man for defending himself, Deputy."

"She was a girl. Not yet eighteen. He raped her first, then finished her off with a knife."

"And where was this supposed to have happened?"

"Denver."

Brothers pulled his feet off the open drawer and sat up in his chair. "That don't sound like Gil, mister. I think maybe you got the wrong man. Not only that, but you're way the hell out of your jurisdiction."

Longarm looked at Brothers and then at his deputy. He did not know if he should accept them as honest lawmen, or as henchmen in the pay of the Lazy M. He squared his shoulders and decided his best bet would be to take the two lawmen at their word and get on after Gil Forman.

"I'll thank you for my gun," he said to Brothers.

"Why? You goin' somewhere?"

"You're damned right. After Gil Forman."

"Afraid that'll have to wait, Long."

"For what?"

"For the trial."

"What trial?"

"Your trial—for the murder of Clem Jagger."

"What the hell are you talking about?"

"You admitted you threw Jagger out that window, didn't you?"

"I told you what happened."

"Well, it looks like you broke the poor son of a bitch's neck. He's as dead as last week's newspaper."

"That won't wash, Brothers. I saw Jagger move after he landed. He didn't have any broken neck, unless you broke it for him."

Brothers jumped up as Colson moved to Longarm's side and then behind him. Longarm turned to deal with Colson, but Brothers stepped quickly around his desk and brought down the barrel of his six-gun. Lights exploded deep within Longarm's skull and he felt his knees turn to rope.

Before he hit the floor, Longarm was unconscious.

Chapter 6

When Longarm came to his senses, he found himself on a cell cot, the moon's light streaming in through a barred window over his head. He sat up at once and immediately wished he hadn't. His head rocked wildly. Feeling at the back of it through his thick hair, his fingers traced a sizable bump ridged with a fresh scab where the gun barrel had broken through. He could live with it, but would have preferred not to have had to.

Reaching gingerly down for his hat on the floor beside the bunk, he got up and walked over to the barred door and looked out. He saw only a dim corridor, a single window at one end, a door to the town marshal's office at the other. There were four other cells besides his, but they were all empty.

He went back to his bunk and sat down, the moonlight pouring over his shoulder, his thoughts chasing each other like a dog chasing its tail. Gil Forman was long gone now, on his way to Canada, more than likely, his foreman probably along with him. Longarm did not believe for an instant Brothers's statement that the fall had broken Jagger's neck, though it would not have bothered him all that much if it had.

He heard the door at the end of the corridor open, then light footsteps hurrying toward his cell. He was standing at the bars, peering out, when Teresa, her face pale and anxious, appeared in the dim corridor before him.

"You're in real trouble, Mr. Long."

"That's not news to me, Teresa. Did you bring a hacksaw blade?"

"I'm serious! They're going to lynch you. I heard them talking in The Bonanza. They're getting themselves all tanked up to come down here and lynch you for Clem Jagger's murder."

"You mean he *is* dead?"

"Nobody really knows, or cares."

"Any excuse—good, bad, or indifferent—is that it?"

"Yes. You walked right into a hornet's nest, Custis Long. Most of these gunslicks are in the pay of the Lazy M. And the rest don't give a damn one way or the other. Most of them are running from the law. Hanging a lawman ain't a crime, the way they look at it."

"I was beginning to figure that out."

"You should have done that before you rode in here all bright and sassy."

"Has anyone gone for the rope yet?"

"Long since. And they'll be coming for you any minute!"

"Then help me get out of here."

She looked at him shrewdly, calculatingly, and he realized she had not come to him solely out of concern for his welfare. "Why should I help you, Mr. Long?"

"I'm innocent."

"That's not enough of a reason, not for me. I've seen plenty of innocent men shot down in cold blood in this town."

"You want to know what's in it for you."

She hesitated a moment, then moistened her lips nervously. "Yes."

"What do you want?"

"I want you to take me from this hellhole."

"That's crazy. If I get out of this mess, I'll be doing some hard riding."

"I don't care. I know how to ride—and shoot, if it comes to that. And I hate this place!"

"I see. You'd like a nicer, more romantic spot. Like San Francisco."

"Yes," she replied eagerly, "or Denver."

Longarm sighed. "Looks like you've got me over a barrel."

She brightened and smiled devilishly. "You take me with you and I'll have you over something else."

"That a promise?"

She nodded eagerly. "Now, what should I do?"

"How'd you get in here?"

"Colson is asleep on his cot inside the office."

"And you just walked in past him."

Her eyes glinted malevolently. "He's out cold. Dead drunk."

"How'd you manage that?"

"I brought him a bottle and entertained him while he was drinking it."

"I see. Well, go back and get the keys to this cell, and bring my six-gun."

She turned and ran lightly down the hallway. He saw her press open the door and then vanish into the office. Listening intently, he thought he heard a light scuffle. A moment later she reappeared in the doorway and hurried toward him, carrying a key ring in one hand, his six-gun in the other.

"I heard a scuffle," he told her.

"He opened his eyes when I was taking the key ring from his belt."

"What'd you do?"

She shuddered slightly. "I clubbed him with your gun."

"Let me have it while you unlock the cell."

She handed his Colt through the bars to him and began trying the keys to find the one that fit. Meanwhile, he checked the revolver's load, then stuck the .44 in his belt and waited not very patiently for Teresa to find the right key.

When at last she did, he pushed open the cell door and preceded her down the corridor. She was about to hurry past him into the office when he threw up his left arm to bar her progress. He had heard movement inside the office. He peered cautiously around the doorjamb and saw Colson standing groggily in the center of the office, a double-barreled Greener in his hand. It was leveled at the doorway, and as soon as he saw Longarm's head poking into the room, he fired. Longarm ducked back in time and saw the wall beside him shred as the heavy buckshot tore into it. Terrified, Teresa stifled a cry.

Poking his gun hand around the doorjamb, Longarm pumped three quick shots into the room. Amid the thunderous reverberations, he heard the Greener thumping to the floor, the sound of a man's body hitting the floor beside it. Cautiously, Longarm peered into the room. Colson was sprawled face down on the floor, partially covering the shotgun, a widening rivulet of blood seeping out from under his body.

Darting into the room, Longarm lifted down his cross-draw rig from a hook and strapped it on. His watch and derringer had been taken from him, and he began looking through the desk drawers for them.

"What are you looking for?" Teresa asked.

"My derringer."

"I saw it. Brothers has it. And your watch, too."

Cursing, Longarm shrugged into his brown jacket and snatched a box of cartridges off a shelf.

"Listen!" Teresa cried, hurrying to the window.

Longarm heard the cries also and peered over her shoulder through the window. With Brothers in the lead, a gun-toting mob was surging down the street, flaring torches casting a lurid glow over the sea of grim, bearded faces. Colson's shotgun blast and his own three shots had thoroughly alerted the men that had been gathering for the lynching, and from the looks of it, they were anxious not to let Longarm escape their rope.

"Oh, my God!" Teresa cried as the mob filled the street in front of the jail. "We're too late!"

"Maybe not," Longarm told her as he slid a beam in place across the door.

He took Teresa's arm and, hurrying from the office, pulled her down the hallway after him to the window. Lifting the sash, he boosted her out into the back alley.

"Get my horse and gear from the stable, and a mount for yourself. I'll meet you in the alley at the north end of town."

"What are you going to do?"

"Stall them. Hurry! Don't let them see you!"

She was gone in an instant, swallowed up in the darkness. Longarm hurried back into the office as heavy boots trampled up onto the low porch accompanied by the thump of heavyset men hurling themselves at the barred door. It was a flimsy door, and Longarm saw the lengthwise boards bending and cracking under the assault, but fortunately the beam held. The shouts of others back in the crowd urging them on came clearly through the door, and Longarm realized that before long a battering ram would be brought up to smash through the door.

Longarm swung the barrel of his six-gun through an unlit kerosene lamp sitting on Brothers's desk. The kerosene splattered across the floor, the base of the lamp following after it, disgorging more kerosene. Longarm lifted the base off the floor and emptied it over a wide area, including the top of the desk. Then he took down a lighted lamp hanging from a nail and flung it onto the floor. With a mighty *whump* the kerosene caught. In an instant the flames raced across the floor, sweeping over

Colson's body, then leapt up the walls and began licking greedily at the front door.

Longarm fired two quick shots through the flaming door. From the other side of it came startled cries of pain and surprise. He sent a third round through one of the windows. There was another sharp outcry as feet pounded frantically back off the porch. With his fore-arm held up to his face to protect his eyes from the roaring flames leaping up the office's tinder-dry walls, Longarm backed from the office and into the cell block. Glancing down the hallway, he saw a townsman's head and shoulders poking through the open window, a big Colt gleaming in his hand.

As Longarm raced toward him, the fellow looked up in surprise and tried to aim the Colt. Longarm smashed the gun out of his hand, lowered his shoulders, and bowled through the window, driving the man back out into the alley, carrying with him a shower of glass. He landed on the townsman, who offered no resistance as Longarm pushed himself erect and raced down the alley. But men at the head of the alley caught sight of Long-arm and darted after him, their quaking torches sending an uncertain light ahead of Longarm. As he ran, he could hear them calling back frantically to their companions.

Longarm saw a doorway that led into the rear of a building. Ducking through it, he found himself in a restaurant's small kitchen. Past the astonished cook he darted, then out the door and across the street into an alley. Keeping in its shadows, he raced along. Behind him he heard growing cries for the formation of a bucket brigade, and glancing back he saw how bright the night sky had become. He had not lost his pursuers, however. They had followed after him into the alley and were still on his tail, every now and then sending a wild shot or two after him.

When one slug came uncomfortably close, Longarm decided to end this nonsense. He ducked into a dark doorway and waited. Two men, one a few strides behind the other and both puffing hard, pounded doggedly past. Longarm stepped out of the doorway and brought down the man in the rear with a blow from his Colt. The fellow's hat went flying, and he cried out as he sagged to the ground. The man in front had spun around, bringing up his revolver. Longarm ducked back into the shadows as the man fired, the flash from his muzzle lancing through the night. Aiming at the muzzle flash, Longarm fired back and heard the round punch into the man's flesh. Gasping in surprise, the fellow crumpled to the ground.

Longarm did not pause to examine either man as he raced on down the alley. Leaving it a few moments later, he was racing out of town, wondering where in the hell Teresa was, when he heard the pound of hooves behind him. Turning, he saw Teresa astride a huge black, bearing down on him, leading his own mount.

She slowed as she overtook him and, bending down, passed his mount's reins to him. He grabbed them and swung into his saddle. At once she lifted her black to a gallop. Clapping his heels to his mount, Longarm followed after her. In a moment they were putting the town behind them as they clattered across a plank bridge, then swept past a ghostly clump of cottonwood on the other side of the creek.

Only then did they pull up to glance back. The far end of Silver Creek was in turmoil. A confused, milling crowd was still trying to contain the fire, which by now had apparently spread to adjacent buildings. From out of the roiling black smoke the flames winked at Longarm like devils' eyes.

There was not a single rider in pursuit.

They turned back around in their saddles and galloped off into the night.

As dawn lightened the eastern sky, Longarm made a dry camp high on a ridge, one that gave him an excellent view of the trail below, and of any pursuers that might still be after them. As Longarm finished unrolling his sugan, Teresa moved close to him. He straightened up and turned to her.

"I know where Gil Forman is," she told him.

"Where?"

"In an abandoned mine north of here."

"What's he doing there?"

"There's a saloon and a few abandoned buildings there. He's there now with Jagger, waiting for word of what happens to you. If you get lynched, he figures it'll be safe for him to go back to his brother's ranch. Otherwise, he'll keep on across the border."

"Who told you this?"

"Pete, the old gent who runs the livery stable. He overheard Brothers and Gil talking while Gil was saddling his mount."

"How come Pete told you?"

"He likes me."

"Enough to let you take my horse and give you that big black?"

"You find that hard to believe?"

"Depends on how old he is. When I left my horse in the livery, he looked pretty far gone to me."

She laughed softly. "Pete's old, but not dead yet. It's been a long time since he tasted someone as young as me."

"That what kept you?"

"I tried not to waste my time. Pete took out his teeth and I unbuttoned my bodice. I never wear a corset." She smiled wickedly. "I don't begrudge the old fool. It did wonders for his morale."

"I can imagine."

She took a step closer. "Can you?"

"How far is this abandoned mine?"

"Half a day's ride," she replied, moving still closer, "maybe a little more."

"Then we better get some shut-eye."

"Yes," she said.

"You . . . don't have a sleeping blanket?"

"All I have is what I am wearing now. I have given up everything for you, Mr. Long."

"Call me Custis."

She was pressed hard against him now, and despite his need for sleep, he found himself responding. She was entirely accurate, of course. All she had given up was being stranded in what she herself described as a hellhole. But she *had* saved his life. In a real sense, he owed her.

And maybe he owed himself, too.

He let his hands drop to her shoulders. As they rested

gently on them, she lifted her face to him. He bent his head and kissed her on the lips. They were hot, pulsing, and opened immediately to the pressure of his lips. In a moment they had both stripped themselves and were scrambling in under the flaps of his sugan to get out of the morning chill.

"Mmm," she murmured, wrapping her long limbs about his thighs. "When I gave old Pete my breast back there, it did wonders for him. For me, it started something a lot deeper."

"You mean you got an itch you want me to scratch."

"Yes, Custis," she said. "Now shut up and get to it."

His big hand dropped to her moist pubis. She sighed and opened her thighs. He plastered his lips onto hers. Clinging to him, she swung her body under his. With his knee, he nudged her thighs wider still. Already her moist pubis had touched the tip of his erection.

"I can feel you! What are you waiting for?"

He chuckled and nudged himself in just slightly. Her fingers flew down his flanks, and with a swift, heated urgency that aroused him even more, she took hold of him in a hasty, frantic effort to guide him still deeper into her. He felt his erection, raw now with desire, burst past her entrance, thrusting full and deep. She moaned from deep within and fastened her lips to his, her tongue probing wildly as she brought her legs up and locked her ankles around his back. With each thrust she hugged him still tighter, her hips grinding, sucking him still deeper into her.

Pulling back mischievously, careful not to come out entirely, he waited a moment, then thrust back in, deeper, this time hitting bottom. He felt Teresa shudder under the impact. She opened her mouth to gasp, her head thrown back, her eyes shut tightly as he continued his long, deep plunges, driving fiercely into her until he felt himself moving inexorably toward his own climax. Tiny, inarticulate cries broke from Teresa's throat. She began twisting her head from side to side. Still deeper he thrust, rocking her violently, slamming into her with such force it felt as if a switch had been turned deep in his groin, catapulting him out of control.

Teresa cried out, a high, keening shriek, and he felt her go rigid under him. Her inner muscles tightened convulsively. He bore in then with a sudden powerful thrust. They came in a long, shuddering orgasm that left Longarm limp, still deep within her warm, clasping pocket, coming again and again in a series of uncontrollable spasms that only gradually subsided.

A blissful sense of relief engulfed him. He fell forward onto her, his shaft still enclosed in her soft, warm snugness, her legs still clasped tightly about his waist. She did not want to let him go, it seemed.

"You came near death this day," she whispered. "So now you feel life surging through you, and I feel it too, flowing into me. It was wonderful, Custis."

"I enjoyed myself, too," he admitted.

"Then don't you dare roll off me now and go to sleep. I am just coming awake to a real man. It does not happen often to a girl in my profession."

He chuckled softly, his face buried in the luxurious abundance of her fragrant hair. "I hear you."

"Good!"

As the first light of dawn streaked the eastern sky, Teresa rolled over onto him, still holding him with her legs. A moment later she was astride him, her head thrown back, the lines of her neck muscles taut and straining. Then she began to raise and lower herself, allowing her inner warmth to caress his erection. At first it had little effect, but she was patient. Slowly at first, but gradually, with maddening deliberation, she increased her pace. Longarm felt the first faint ache of a new urgency growing within his loins. It was not long before he felt himself growing larger, surging upward into her. Moaning, Teresa increased her tempo, driving deeper now with each thrust, impaling herself eagerly on Longarm's thrusting erection with a fierce, reckless abandon.

He reached up to cup her breasts in his big, rough hands. She nodded her head frantically. Yes! She wanted that. Longarm could feel her erect nipples, hard as bullets, thrusting against the palms of his hands. Her movements became more violent now, but no longer was she thrusting up and down. She was moving back and forth along the length of his erection, turning it to fire. He cried out at the sudden urgency that flared in his loins, and she grinned down at him, blowing a wet lock of hair off her face. He dropped his hands from her breasts and grabbed her hips to increase the pace of her horizontal thrusting—nearing his climax now, frantic she not pull all the way off.

"Faster!" she told him, her voice hoarse and deep with need. "Faster! And deeper! Damn you!"

He did his best to oblige, and suddenly she flung herself forward onto him, her thick veil of hair falling over him, her lips fastening to his. He opened his mouth and her tongue darted frantically in, flicking like a snake's tongue. In an agony of desire, he flung up his buttocks, driving so deep and violently into her that he nearly catapulted her over his shoulders.

She laughed, then cried out in the pure wild joy of it, and he let go of her hips then and encircled her shoulders, still holding his mouth hard against hers, their tongues entwined now in a lewd embrace of their own. Her hips were grinding down on him now with a control that was as amazing as it was effective, achieving a synchronization that both excited and astonished him. They were welded together in a fierce, passionate dance that had become sheer instinct. In a wild but perfectly controlled rhythm his hips slammed up to meet each one of her down-thrusts.

Abruptly there came the inevitable, headlong rush to climax. He felt himself exploding deep within her. She flung her head back and cried out again as she too climaxed, her inner muscles opening and contracting, pulling at his erection. Clinging to each other, shuddering, they let the storm gradually subside, until at last she collapsed, laughing in delight, onto his rock-like chest.

Her face in the morning light gleamed with perspiration. Panting, she raised her face to look full into his eyes, then covered his face with soft, playful kisses. She was in a transport of delight. And this pleased Longarm as much as it pleased her. When she slid off him finally, it was slowly, lingeringly.

"That was so nice," she told him softly, brushing his damp locks off his forehead.

"You did seem to enjoy it."

"When it is a business—that is, when you are lying

on your back allowing dirty men to plow you with drunken abandon—when you are simply hauling ashes, in other words—believe me, Custis, you lose some of your enthusiasm."

"I can imagine that."

"It becomes drearily mechanical. But in a way, that's good. You no longer care and you no longer want to. Caring for such men would be fatal. But every once in a while you wonder what it would be like to find a man with whom you could really let loose."

"You let loose this time, all right."

"It was fun. The way it used to be. To please us I used all I have learned. And it worked. I wonder now if I could ever go back to that sad profession. It's a good living, I suppose, if you put something by for a rainy day. But something in me was beginning to die."

"That's why you wanted out of Silver Creek."

"Yes. And out of the life. Thank you, Custis, for helping me."

"I should be thanking you. I'd be dancing from a noose right now if you hadn't come for me."

"Then you won't abandon me. I have only the clothes on my back, and this horse."

"That's a fine piece of horseflesh, and those duds should last until we get back to Silver Creek."

"You mean you're going back there!"

"When the time comes. Don't worry. I won't abandon you, Teresa."

She kissed him again, then moved her long, silken limbs close against his under the sugan's blanket. He turned his face away from the rising sun and closed his eyes. She had turned his limbs to sodden logs. Despite the happy chatter of the birds greeting the new dawn, he closed his eyes and felt himself drift off.

Teresa's hand closed about his and a moment later he was asleep.

They reached the abandoned mine late that same day. Huddled in a narrow canyon below it were a few ramshackle buildings split by a dirt road that went on through. There was the saloon Teresa had mentioned, the shell of a general store alongside it, and across the road from that, a two-story building with hardly a single window intact. Against the nearby mountainside, he made out the yellow scars of mine dumps and the scaffolding of buildings stripped of their covering timber. The crumbling skeleton of a stamping mill stood out starkly on the slope, close by what had been the mine's entrance.

Leaving Teresa in the rocks with their mounts, Longarm surveyed the place. Perched on a ridge high above the saloon, he caught the dim scuff of movement and the low mutter of voices coming from the building across the road from the saloon. A man passed out of the saloon and crossed to the building, disappearing behind it. He was about as tall as Gil Forman, but the angle was such that it had not been possible for Longarm to identify him for sure. Four dusty horses stood patiently at the hitch rail in front of the saloon. Behind the saloon there was a horse barn, and from it Longarm could hear the occasional stamping of horses, and from the saloon's back yard every now and then came the squawk of foraging chickens.

Longarm hunkered down to wait.

98

In about ten minutes two men strode from the saloon, mounted up, and rode out, heading north to the border. Longarm was afraid these two might possibly be Gil Forman and Clem Jagger, but as they rode past him on their way out of town, he got a much better glimpse of them and saw they were strangers. From the furtive look on their scarred, ferret-like faces, they were more than likely outlaws on the run.

That left two horses at the hitch rail. Longarm waited another half hour or so, then returned to the waiting Teresa.

"They're still down there. And I think I know where."

"You're going in after them?"

He nodded, checking the load in his .44. He felt almost naked without his vest-pocket derringer, and mentally cursed Brothers for taking it.

He handed Teresa his Winchester. "Can you use this?"

She nodded.

"Are you sure?"

"Yes, Custis. I am sure."

"All right, then. I'll leave it with you to protect yourself and the horses if this goes bad."

"Thank you."

He looked at her and saw the light in her eyes and realized how much she was enjoying this. "I won't be long," he told her. "I want to get this over with before it gets dark."

"Are you going to arrest both men?"

"Only Gil—if I can."

"And if you can't?"

Longarm shrugged. "I'll cross that bridge when I come to it."

"It's true what they say, isn't it, that you don't have a warrant for Gil Forman's arrest?"

"True enough."

"Then is any of this legal?"

"Not much of it, I suppose. But neither was that attempt back there to lynch me on a trumped-up murder charge."

He left her then, working his way back to the ledge he had perched on before. Once he reached it, he paused to check on any movement below him. As he watched, the saloon keeper ducked out of the saloon to empty a slops jar, then disappeared back inside. There was little activity after that. But Longarm could hear the sound of pans clattering in the saloon's kitchen.

The sun, a huge red ball, hung just over the peaks as he angled down the shale-littered slope and came out behind the saloon. Chickens squawked and fluttered in outrage at his sudden appearance. Sidestepping a fat Rhode Island red, he strode into the saloon's kitchen, his Colt out.

A squat, flat-faced Indian woman looked up from a coal-black wood stove. He nodded to her and kept on through the small kitchen and came out into the saloon. The saloon's owner had heard him coming and was reaching for a shotgun under the bar. Longarm waggled his Colt at him. The man released the shotgun and stepped back. Seen up close, he was a large, balding, round-faced fellow with a black patch over one eye.

"No need for that shotgun," Longarm told him. "Stay out of this and you'll live to eat your supper."

"You a lawman?"

Longarm opened his wallet and flashed his badge. "I'm looking for Gil Forman."

The owner of the saloon shrugged.

"Where is he?"

"This is your party, mister."

"Those two mounts outside. They must belong to somebody."

"Can't argue with that."

"Get out from behind the bar."

The burly man did as Longarm told him. Longarm reached in under the bar for the shotgun. Breaking it open, he let the shells slip out, then tossed the gun to the floor and stepped out the saloon door, heading for the building behind which he had earlier watched a man disappear. He was halfway across the road when he heard a mean chuckle coming from the corner of the saloon. Turning, he saw Clem Jagger step into view, his six-gun out and leveled on Longarm's chest.

"You lookin' for someone, Deputy?" he snarled, his yellow fangs flashing against his unshaven face.

"That's right, Jagger. Gil Forman."

Jagger cocked his gun and lifted it to sight along the barrel. "I don't know how you got out of Silver Creek, you son of a bitch, but you ain't got a chance in hell of gettin' out of this."

Longarm saw the sudden, cold resolve in the man's face as his finger tightened about the trigger, and was about to throw himself to one side when a rifle's sharp crack came from above. As the detonation reverberated about the canyon's walls, the six-gun fell from Jagger's hand and he pitched forward to the ground, a neat hole punched in his back. Glancing up, Longarm saw Teresa outlined clearly in the setting sun. She was standing on the ridge where he had stationed himself before, slowly lowering his smoking Winchester. She sure as hell *did* know how to use it.

He waved quickly at her, then turned to run across the road. A shot rang out from an upstairs window in the building opposite him. The ground erupted at his feet. It kicked up twice more as he ducked back to the corner of the saloon and flattened himself against the wall.

He peered around the corner of the saloon at the second-floor window and thought he saw in one of them the faint glow of a cigarette tip. Not until it winked out did he realize it was only the sun's last rays glancing off a splinter of glass. As soon as the sun dipped below the surrounding peaks, darkness seeped into the canyon like smoke, obscuring the building almost immediately. In no hurry at all, he waited for it to grow still darker, confident that Gil could go nowhere, not with his mount still stamping wearily at the hitch rail in front of the saloon.

At last, with an impenetrable river of darkness flowing through the canyon, Longarm darted across the road and cut around to the rear of the building. Spotting a door, he pushed it open, stepped inside, and found himself facing a narrow flight of stairs. He cocked his head to listen. The smell of an abandoned place came to him, musty and dry, with the remnant odors of a thousand items once held within it still clinging to the walls and flooring. The tiny, scurrying feet of a rat crossed a hidden beam above him. That was the only sound. Nothing came from the building, from the road on the other side of it, or from the saloon.

But he could sense Gil Forman crouched in the darkness on the floor above.

He set one foot forward and down, testing the flooring in front of the stairwell, letting his weight fall easy and slow, and found there was no flooring, only solid, hard-packed ground. He kept going until his foot struck the first step. He eased himself up onto it and then, testing each board, slowly mounted the stairs until he reached the second-floor landing. An open doorway's dim, rectangular opening yawned before him. He was moving cautiously along the landing when the toe of his right boot struck the doorsill.

Crouching quickly, he waited for the sound to fade, but small as the echo was, it seemed to swell ominously into the room beyond. He listened intently, his mouth open slightly, but heard nothing. Even so, he could still feel the waiting man crouched in the room's darkness. He kept himself perfectly still and waited.

A voice, hoarse now and no longer carrying the surly arrogance Longarm remembered, came at him from the gloom beyond the doorway. "That you, Long?"

"It's me, all right. Throw down your gun and come out of there."

"You killed Clem."

"He's dead enough, all right."

"It was Teresa. I saw the whole thing. You got that hot bitch on your side!"

"Looks like it."

"You think the two of you can take me all the way back to Denver?"

"We can sure as hell try."

"This is crazy, Long. I didn't do nothin' to that girl."

"Then a trial should make that clear."

"Damn you! You know what'll happen to me at a trial. But I didn't kill her, Long! I didn't."

Gil's voice echoed hollowly in the empty room so that it was impossible for Longarm to tell where the man stood, if indeed he was standing and not crouched in some corner. The darkness outside was complete by this time and no light at all filtered through the windows. Edging himself through the doorway, Longarm held his Colt out in front of him, his eyes straining to pick out Gil Forman in the nearly impenetrable darkness.

"She was no good, that kid! I tell you, Long, she was a wild one. She wouldn't let a man be. She wasn't no angel."

"Don't matter, Gil. You had no right to do that to her!"

"But I didn't!"

Softly, keeping his head low, Longarm said, "Then drop your gun and come out of here quietly. Maybe the judge will see it your way."

A shot lanced out of the darkness, the round smashing into the floor at Longarm's feet and whining off to bury itself in the wall. A second shot came after it, this one whispering past Longarm's cheek to slam into the stairwell behind him.

Throwing himself flat, Longarm aimed at the source of the two gun flashes and fired, his finger pulsing automatically as the double-action .44 jumped in his hand, the flash from his gun barrel blooming blue-crimson in the blackness. Somewhere in the heart of the racket, Longarm heard Gil cry out, and ceased firing. He heard a heavy gun slam to the floor, then the shallow, slow guttering of Gil Forman's breathing and the scrape of his jacket as his back slid down a wall.

Longarm went forward cautiously. His foot struck the man's six-gun. He kicked it out of the way and continued on until he found himself looking down at the sprawled figure of Gil Forman, his face only a pale shine in the dark room. On one knee beside him, Longarm rested the barrel of his gun on the man's temple.

"Can you hear me, Gil?"

As if from a long distance, Gil replied, "Yes, I can hear you, you bastard."

"Admit it. You killed her."

Gil smiled. "It's all over for me, Long. But it ain't for you. You killed the wrong man."

"Did I now?"

"It was Matt killed that tramp."

"You expect me to believe that?"

"He was in Denver that week, banking some money. It's the truth, Long."

Longarm felt a little sick. "Go on."

"I told him about the girl. He didn't believe what I said, but she sure made a believer out of him . . ."

Gil's voice had been getting more scratchy, distant. Longarm waited patiently, then urged him to finish. Moistening dried lips, Gil went on, "The fool kid . . . she got rough with Matt, pulled a gun on him. Matt went wild. I came in with him sitting there on the bed, looking at her . . ."

"Is that all of it?"

"It's the truth, Long," he whispered urgently. "I ain't in no position to lie now, not where I'm headed. I told Matt to get out of Denver, that no one knew he was in town. I told him I'd handle it."

"And now you tell me."

Gil's laugh was low, barely audible. "I wanted you to know . . . you killed an innocent man."

"And for that you turned in your own brother."

"Don't give me that shit, Long!" Gil said, lifting his head to peer wildly into Longarm's eyes. "Matt's safe now! I took care of that like I promised. With me dead . . . there's no way you can tie Matt to Aleta Crowley!"

With these words, uttered in a hoarse, furious snarl, he slumped back to the floor, his head cracking against the bare wood. For a moment he stirred slowly, struggling, it seemed, to get more words out, and then with a kind of deep, shuddering sigh, he stiffened and lay perfectly still. Longarm leaned his head forward, resting his ear on the man's chest. There was no heartbeat. Shaking the man's shoulder, he felt only a slack looseness.

Longarm stood up, holstered his .44, and left the room. Outside in the cool evening, he became aware of tiny beads of cold sweat standing out on his forehead. He had begun listening to Gil Forman with no thought that he could believe anything the man said. But when Gil was done talking, Longarm knew he had spoken the truth.

Gil was right. Longarm had killed the wrong man.

Teresa, still carrying his rifle, stepped out of the inky

shadows surrounding the building. "I heard shots," she said. "Are you all right?"

"I'm all right."

"What about Forman?"

"He's still up there—and he won't be coming down."

She stopped before him, her face a pale oval in the darkness, staring up at him. "Then you've accomplished what you came for. You'll be going back now, to Denver."

"I suppose."

As they started up the dirt road, the barkeep and his squat Indian woman stepped out of the saloon. The man was carrying a lantern. He watched Longarm and Teresa continue on, then headed across to the empty building. As he disappeared behind it, the Indian woman knelt by Clem Jagger's body, took off her wool wrap, and draped it over the man's head and shoulders.

They made camp high above the mine, and close to midnight Longarm came awake to the sound of hoofbeats as two riders below them on the road came up from the south and kept on until they reached the saloon. The men did not linger long there, galloping back the way they had come almost immediately, undoubtedly taking back to Silver Creek the news that Matt Forman's brother was dead, along with Clem Jagger.

Teresa raised her head and looked sleepily at him. "Anything wrong?"

"Riders on the trail below. They're gone now."

She let her head drop back onto her saddle and was

asleep almost at once, but Longarm remained awake, staring up the starlit sky, considering the significance of this day's work, and the dying words of Gil Forman.

Maybe he wasn't going to be heading straight back to Denver, after all.

Chapter 7

Late the next afternoon they rode into Silver Creek. By the time they reached the middle of town the sidewalks were lined with sullen gunslicks who had halted in their tracks to watch the two ride in. As a result of the fire Longarm had set, the town marshal's office and jail were now a black tangle of beams and roofing, and the two buildings adjoining it were gutted almost as thoroughly, with only the rear wall of one still standing.

They put their horses into the hitch rail in front of The Bonanza and dismounted. Teresa untied her saddlebags and moved ahead of him up the saloon's porch steps. Longarm had already discussed with Teresa what to do, and as he mounted the steps behind her, she hurried ahead of him into the saloon, heading for her room upstairs to pack her possibles. Shouldering through the surly ranks of men crowding onto the porch, Longarm followed Teresa into the saloon, strode over to the bar, and rested his foot on the brass foot rail.

"Whiskey," he told the barkeep.

The man looked unhappily past Longarm at the men surging into the saloon after him, obviously hoping for one of them to tell him what to do. When no help came from that quarter, the barkeep unstoppered a fresh bottle and poured Longarm's drink. Then he left the bottle at Longarm's elbow and moved a good six feet down the bar.

Longarm tipped the glass up and let the raw whiskey scour a path down his gullet, taking most of the day's trail dust with it. Then he wiped off his mouth with the back of his hand and turned to survey the sullen crowd still working its way closer to him, forming a ragged crescent with him at the center, the bar at his back. Longarm watched the men coolly, not bothering to hide his contempt.

There was a commotion at the door and Brothers entered the saloon, promptly pushing through the crowd toward Longarm. When he stood finally in front of Longarm, the tall lawman saw that Brothers's right arm was in a sling. He remembered those blind shots he had fired through the door and window, and was pleased that one of those rounds, at least, had found a proper target.

"Damn you, Long! You killed my deputy."

"It was self-defense, and I have a witness to prove it."

"You were in my custody. You broke out! You can't call that self-defense."

"Sure, I can, since the charges were trumped-up.

Clem Jagger didn't have a broken back, after all, Brothers. Fact is, he showed up not far from here, covering me with a six-gun."

This was obviously not a surprise to Brothers, which meant those riders Longarm had heard had indeed raced back here with the news, news that was already on its way to Matt Forman, Longarm had no doubt.

He saw the town marshal swallow hard, searching for some kind of adequate response. "You must be crazy," he blustered finally, "comin' back here!"

"Well, the thing is Teresa left town in a hurry. She's upstairs now, getting a few things." Longarm poured himself a second drink, downed it, then turned back around to face Brothers. "And as a matter of fact, I've come back to get something myself."

"Yeah?" the town marshal sneered. "And what might that be?"

"My watch and derringer. I understand you took it off me after you stiffed me."

The man's eyes narrowed. "You think it's going to be that easy to get it back, do you?"

Longarm drew his Colt effortlessly and thrust its muzzle into Brothers's soft stomach. The man paled. Smiling thinly, Longarm reached past Brothers's arm sling and yanked back his coat. Looping his finger through the chain, Longarm lifted the watch and derringer from the man's vest and dropped them into his own side pocket.

At that moment, carrying bulging saddlebags and a blanket roll, Teresa hurried down the stairs at the back

111

of the saloon, then pushed her way through the crowd and out the door.

Longarm holstered his Colt, turned back to the bar, and poured himself another drink.

"Damn your eyes, Long," Brothers snarled. "You ain't heard the last of this."

"Sure I have, unless you want to brace me right here." He smiled easily at the town marshal. "I see you got a bum left arm, so I'll let you draw first. At this distance it won't make much difference who gets off the first shot."

Brothers's face went pale. "You callin' me?" He took an uneasy step back, as did those crowding close behind him.

"That's up to you," Longarm told him.

Brothers swallowed. "Hell, Long, this ain't my fight, it's Matt Forman's. I'll let him deal with you."

That was about the response Longarm had expected. He spun a coin onto the bar, then pushed himself roughly through the crush of unwashed men. There was not a gunslick in that room who did not want to reach for his sidearm and blast Longarm. But these were men who preferred to execute their enemies with a shotgun blast in the back, most of the time from the mouth of a dark alley. Facing down an armed man in broad daylight was completely out of their ken.

Shouldering through the bat-wings, Longarm saw that Teresa, wearing a split skirt, had finished tying down her blanket roll and saddlebags, and was already astride her big black. He nodded to her and she backed the horse from the hitch rail and started down the street.

Stepping up into his saddle, he swung his horse around and followed her out of town.

He did not bother to look back.

When Longarm and Teresa rode into the Circle T two days later, Tom Goodnight—a somber Ellen Buckman at his side—welcomed them warmly, insisting they stay over for the night.

Surprised to find Ellen at the Goodnight ranch, Longarm inquired after Buckman's condition at the first opportunity, and learned that Ellen's father had died soon after reaching Placer Town, despite Doc Wolfson's best efforts. Later, at supper, Longarm told them of his and Teresa's adventures in the mining town of Silver Creek, and of Gil Forman's and Clem Jagger's deaths. When he had finished, Longarm could not help noting the cold gleam of satisfaction in Ellen's eyes at the news of Gil Forman's death. With the meal done, the two women strolled off into the gathering dusk to get acquainted, while Longarm and Goodnight eased into wicker chairs on the front veranda.

Goodnight accepted one of Longarm's last cheroots, then leaned back and puffed a while. Then, with a sigh, he said, "I am afraid the death of Ellen's father was a signal to the other hill ranchers."

"How's that, Tom? You mean things are worse than when I rode out?"

"They are that. I tried to get help from the other cattlemen, but they didn't have the stomach for it. Now, with the death of Ellen's father, things have gone from bad to worse. Buckman had done his best to convince

113

the other hill ranchers not to follow Matt Forman's lead. With his voice still, the rest of the hill ranchers are falling into line."

"How bad is it?"

"In two nights three outfits have lost sizable chunks of their herds. Already their owners are thinking of pulling out."

Longarm puffed on his cheroot for a few moments, then said, "If what you say is true, the burnout must be pretty damn crowded with freshly rustled cattle."

Goodnight nodded gloomily. "It is that. The Double O lost almost fifty head last night."

"Then I suggest you ride in there and get them."

Goodnight laughed shortly, bitterly. "Easier said than done."

"I didn't say it would be easy. But does that mean it's impossible?"

"You've never seen the place, have you."

"No, I haven't, but Kate Summerfield gave me a pretty good description of it."

"Well, she should know, seeing as how she and Matt Forman are going to be married."

"I wouldn't put much stock in it."

"Well, that's beside the point, anyway. The heart of the problem, Longarm, is that once inside that hellish tangle of vines and alders, it is damn near impossible to find your way out."

"Matt Forman and his men seem to have no problem."

"Matt Forman's a very clever man, Longarm. As he and his men ride in with rustled cattle, they drop off men at strategic points to guide them on the way out.

And each time Matt uses the burnout, as I understand it, he uses a different route."

"If he's got cattle in there now, that means he's got men stationed inside the burnout, at each of those strategic locations. Right?"

"I suppose so. Yes."

"Which means all we have to do is replace their men with our own."

"Our own?"

"Sure. Why not?"

Goodnight stared at Longarm. The idea was so simple and direct, so purely feasible, that he broke into a grin. "Damn it, Longarm, you're right. We could do that."

"Another thing," Longarm said. "I'm a federal officer, but in Montana Territory, I have only limited jurisdiction. Maybe you could raise a posse and put me in charge."

"You mean you'd be willing to lead a posse comitatus?"

"Do you see any problem in raising it?"

"Not after the way them folks around Alder Gulch took care of Plummer and his gang a few years back."

Longarm had been thinking the same thing. In 1864, a hastily formed committee of vigilance had rounded up members of a gang of road agents and murderers led by Sheriff Henry Plummer. In a few weeks Plummer had been strung up, along with two dozen of his outlaws.

"With you leading us," Goodnight continued, "it should be possible for us to get enough men. Double O riders will join us, I'm sure. And maybe I can get the other cattlemen and their crews to throw in with us too."

"Then I say we do it. Besides," confided Longarm, "I'd appreciate the chance to operate in this territory legally as a peace officer."

"Any reason in particular?"

"Yes, Tom. But you don't need to know what that is."

"I'll ride out first thing tomorrow morning, sound out the Double O and the other cattlemen. I think they'll go along. In fact, I'm almost sure of it."

"Meanwhile, I suggest you send out riders to watch the burnout, make sure the cattle inside are still there when it comes time for us to move."

Goodnight frowned. "I hate to do that, Longarm. Look what happened to Biff and Willy."

"Send me, then."

"You itchin' for trouble, are you?"

"I'd like the chance to look this burnout over. One man can stay hidden without too much difficulty, it's two or more men that tend to raise dust."

"If you insist."

"Give me directions and I'll move out tomorrow."

"Done."

Longarm sat back in the wicker chair. Tom Goodnight sounded hopeful, his enthusiasm reflecting Longarm's own confidence. In fact, it was the only course open to Goodnight and the other cattlemen, other than to turn tail and abandon their lands to Matt Forman and his fellow rustlers.

For his part, Longarm had heard a lot about this famous burnout. Now he would get a chance to see it for himself.

• • •

By noon the next day Longarm was on his way, having bid good-bye to Teresa with the understanding that she would wait for him in Placer Town with Ellen. He was at great pains to assure Teresa that he would indeed join her for that trip to Denver, but he got the distinct impression she was worried he would not make it back to keep his promise.

The burnout, as Tom Goodnight explained, was well north of his ranch, on a high plateau ringed by jagged peaks. Directed to a trail just inside the pass, Longarm kept on it steadily, the sun warming his back. He was soon deep in the hills and presently the trail took him across a long, narrow meadow. He saw no sign of any cattle grazing on it and continued on deeper into the hills until he was once again in high timber.

It was old, first-growth pine, massive at the butt and rising in a flawless line toward a high green canopy, the wind sighing in the branches like a distant surf. There was little underbrush, and at certain angles he was able to see a hundred or two hundred yards. The air was blue-shadowed and still, heavy with the tang of pine, and occasionally bright with the call of birds.

He followed the rutted remnants of a wagon road for a while, and later came upon the sad ruins of a log-and-shake cabin. Near it was a square patch of ground enclosed by stakes. Centered in the patch a weathered grave marker lay rotting upon the earth. A pine stood hard by, an ax embedded in the bark. The story was clear: A man had buried his wife or child, and then buried his ax into the pine, and walked off without looking back.

Longarm kept on, and by degrees the country roughened and the pines grew smaller. Ravines gaped before him. He held to the crest of ridges for as long as possible, then dropped into the ravines, crossed over, and rose to the next ridge, the late-afternoon sun dropping steadily in a cloudless sky. Near sunset the trees momentarily opened before him, and he faced a creek running quickly over its stones. Beyond the creek the trees again marched toward the heights.

He kept within the timber, long watching the upper and lower reaches of the creek and the timber on the other side. When he was satisfied he was alone, he rode to the water's edge, let the horse have a long drink, and forded. Twenty yards inside the timber he came to a trail looping stiffly up the side of the mountain. Since there was no other way, he took this.

He rose steadily with the short switchback courses, higher and higher along the edge of the cliff as daylight slowly faded out of the sky. He arrived at last to a leveling-off place, gave the timbered slope below him one last look, and kept himself moving on toward the peaks. Within fifteen minutes the trail brought him to a complete standstill at the edge of a precipice running three hundred feet or more downward into a canyon whose bottom was already dim with night shadows.

The land was deceptive. He had marched out of one canyon to these heights, and now faced another canyon. He had worked himself to a high plateau, an island of rock surrounded by cold space. Night wind began to flow off the peaks still looming above him, soft but cold, and as he peered into the canyon below him, he saw the tide of darkness slowly drown out its floor. A pathway dropped along the face of the precipice, running lower and lower until he could no longer see its course.

There was undoubtedly a better way of moving off this ridge. One end of it was probably anchored against the peaks, providing him with a level route. But an icy wind was freshening at this altitude, it was growing rapidly darker, and he wanted a more sheltered spot for his camp. He urged the horse over the brink of the precipice and down onto the descending ledge.

The cliff side was composed of old, weathered rock, with some vegetation clinging to it. The trail itself was no more than three or four feet wide, sometimes tightening against the cliff, causing his leg to scrape occasionally against the rock as he descended. His mount, meanwhile, was both tired and doubtful of the trail, and frequently stopped, so that Longarm had to use his heels to force the animal on. The narrow trail at times pitched downward so steeply that the horse's front feet slid along the loose dirt and pebbles, and the farther the trail dropped, the blacker it became, until there was no view above Longarm and nothing for him to see below the trail, as a smothering darkness settled over him.

He had gone a hundred feet or so when the horse stopped and refused to go on. He bent forward over its neck and fixed his eyes on the ledge before him until he thought he saw the continuation of the trail. He urged the horse on again. The animal gathered its feet close together and began to proceed with infinite care, moving forward and down in little mincing shifts. Longarm felt his shoulder brushing close against a solid face of rock and felt the animal under him turning slowly until it had completely reversed its direction. Then, heading downward with somewhat more confidence, it moved on.

Looking back and down, Longarm was only barely able to make out the turnaround the horse had sensed, and realized how completely his eyes had failed him. It gave him pause and more than a twinge of uncertainty. But he was committed now to this descent and had no choice but to go on. Less than halfway down a cliff whose total drop could well be three hundred feet or more, turning around to go back was out of the question. Leaning back in the saddle to ease the animal's burden somewhat, he slackened the reins, having no other course, he now realized, but to trust the horse's instinct, and its own impulse for survival.

The animal kept on slowly, steadily, stopping occasionally to blow, but keeping on, all the while the darkness about Longarm growing so profound he felt as if he were descending the inside of a soot-filled chimney.

Without warning, the horse halted and made no effort to go on.

Longarm waited a few moments, peering beyond the horse's flickering ears at the nothingness that yawned before him. But the inky blackness swam like something substantial as his eyes fought to bring out of the gloom some image, some notion of what lay ahead. He gave this up at last and sat back in his saddle, content to wait for the horse to move. He waited a full two minutes, he judged. Then, knowing that something stood in the way, he dismounted with the utmost care and inched past the horse—crowded between it and the canyon wall—his hands holding tightly to the reins.

Once in front of the horse, he got carefully down on

his hands and knees and used his hands to explore the ledge just in front of him. His fingers dug into a sudden, damp barrier of rock and soil sitting on the ledge in front of him. The trail was blocked by a landslide.

He stood up, running his arm forward along the wall in an attempt to judge the extent and depth of the barrier. What he found was that a wet spot in the cliff wall just above the ledge had collapsed onto it. The slide was a new one, not yet packed firm. He ran his hands shovel-like into the dirt and found himself able to move it. Crouching, he began to throw some of the debris off the ledge into the void below him. He heard the rocks and clumps of soil strike after a considerable delay against the sides of the cliff, coming to rest later, dimly, upon the canyon floor.

It took him at least an hour to clear the barrier, and when he stood up again, his hands were bruised and raw from the sharp rocks he had been forced to lift off the trail and hurl into the canyon. He estimated he had cleared a trail through the landslide at least five feet long and three feet wide. Catching up the horse's reins, he led it cautiously forward. Fifty feet brought him to an uncertain spot, and he stopped and crawled on his hands and knees, exploring the ground ahead until he realized he had come to another sharp turnaround. He let the horse take its time folllowing after him as he made the turn on foot and continued the descent.

After a while he could hear the sound of water flowing through the canyon far below him, and not long after, its cold dampness began to reach him. He kept on and the dampness increased along with the sound of the rushing water. He had been on this descent for what seemed an interminable time, and was anxious to put it behind him. But he forced himself to move on only with the greatest caution, walking with a short forward step, surer of himself as the canyon floor appeared nearer.

The horse halted. He saw no reason for it and tugged on the horse impatiently. When he got it moving again, he stepped forward, but his foot found nothing solid to plant on. Losing his balance, he plunged forward into emptiness. His grip tightened convulsively on the reins, and as he swung forward, one foot still on the trail, the weight of his sudden grasp caught the horse by surprise.

It reacted to the sudden pressure with a startled upward fling of its head. Still clinging to the reins, Longarm whipped himself around as he swung outward into space, his other foot slipping off the trail. His chest slammed into the side of the cliff face. Near panic now, the horse moved backward, dragging Longarm along the sharp edge of the trail, the rocks sawing violently at his ribs. Managing to hook one elbow over the ledge, Longarm let go of the reins, anchored himself with both elbows, then boosted himself back up onto the trail. He rested a moment, then rolled over and sat upright.

He glanced up at the horse. It was standing in the blackness, barely visible to Longarm. He thought he caught the gleam of its trembling flanks.

"Thanks, horse," he told it. "You did just fine."

The horse stamped its front feet and began to shake its head, the jingling of its bit echoing brightly in the canyon.

"Don't be so modest," Longarm insisted.

He got up and walked cautiously back along the ledge, shuffling his feet with infinite care until he reached the break in it. He got down once more on his hands and knees, stretched his arm outward, and found nothing. He sat back a moment, drawing a long breath, and then flattened on his belly and inched forward until he teetered on the edge like a balancing board. He reached out again, but was still unable to find anything solid to grab onto.

Pulling back, he found a couple of small rocks and threw the first one at least three feet ahead of him. It bounced once, then clattered down the rest of the cliff face to the canyon floor. He sent another rock after the first one, throwing it harder. This one bounced on the trail on the other side of the gap, and Longarm judged the width of the gap to be at least six feet.

He sat back, exasperated, but not yet defeated. Grabbing a handful of rocks, he dropped them one by one over the edge of the trail, listening to see how long it took for them to reach the canyon floor, and tried to visualize the distance. But he could get no clear idea of the distance remaining between the trail and the canyon floor.

As a last resort, he struck a match and held it cupped in his hands, close against the cliff wall. He saw enough before the match guttered out to give him hope. Only the outer margin of the trail was gone. The inner portion, that part hugging the wall, remained intact, leaving a very narrow path, one that was just barely negotiable. Whether or not the horse could make it, he was not sure. He lit another match, and before it went out decided that, with some luck, the horse would be able to follow across after him.

He rose and tested the ledge's footing, running his

hands along the face of the cliff to give himself direction. His foot struck a rock large enough to cause trouble, and he stooped to dig it out and throw it off the trail. Then he approached the horse, took off its saddle, and carried it across the break, his cheek resting against the cool wall of rock as he moved. Dumping the saddle onto the trail, he returned to the horse, caught up its reins, and led the animal forward, grasping the extreme end of the reins. Halfway out onto the narrow remnant of the trail, he turned to pull on the reins, yanking gently, calling softly to the horse as he did so. It had already proven itself to be a surefooted brute, but it was now also a very wary horse, and when it came to the break, it stopped.

Longarm returned to the horse, inched past its neck, and used the pressure of his body to shift the animal nearer to the wall. He moved out ahead of the horse again and pulled on the reins a second time. This time the horse took a firm step forward, and then another. As soon as it was beyond the initial break, Longarm dropped the reins to allow the horse to lower its head and see the trail for itself. The horse thrust its muzzle downward, breathing and snorting tentatively against the narrow strip of ledge under its feet, then placed a wary forefoot down in front of it, and a moment later advanced the other front foot.

Longarm could hear the animal's flanks dragging along the rock face. Speaking gently to the horse, he reached out his hand to it. Suddenly the horse's hind foot, too close to the edge, slid downward, and the horse made a quick lunge that carried it all the way across to firm ground. The surge caught Longarm by surprise and he jumped back, stumbled, and fell backward, his left hand striking the ledge and then slipping off it. He fought to keep his balance, and just managed to prevent himself from tumbling off into space.

Trembling slightly, he got to his feet, found the saddle, and slapped it back onto the horse and made a loose tie. A cold wind scoured down the canyon, but his face was sticky, and when he took off his hat, beads of sweat streamed down his face. He felt its salt on his lips. Taking up the reins once more, he led the horse downward, taking each step with infinite caution. He was by this time completely exhausted, as much from the natural weariness caused by a full day's ride as by the accumulating tension of this excruciating descent.

He reached the canyon floor at last without further incident, the trail playing out through gravel and chunks of rock. Soon he could feel, as well as hear, the river thundering abreast of him in the darkness far to the right. He kept on until he reached the river and saw the moon's dim glow on its black, glassy surface. The gravel alongside the river churned under his feet, and his horse stumbled and stopped. Longarm pulled it on until he reached a grassy spot that provided better footing. Here Longarm unsaddled the horse again and put hobbles on it. Moving off, he found a high, grass-covered knoll and put down his sugan.

Once inside it, he rested his head back against his saddle, closed his eyes, and was almost instantly asleep.

What woke Longarm close to dawn was a stone grinding with malignant force into his back. He rolled away from it and, blinking the grit out of his eyes, looked about him at the cliff sides dimly visible on all sides. As the sky brightened, Longarm stood up and glanced over at the creek.

Recalling what Tom Goodnight had told him the day before, Longarm realized the burnout would be almost a day's ride further on, which meant he had better mount up and get moving. Goodnight had mentioned a butte overlooking the burnout, and Longarm needed to reach it undetected and wait there for Goodnight's forces to arrive.

He rolled up his bedding and saddled up, having decided to make a campfire at a less-exposed site. He nooned on a ridge, then found himself following another canyon through the afternoon. A couple of hours or so before dusk, he had dismounted, and was letting his horse drink its fill at the broad stream cutting through the high canyon, when he glanced up at the canyon rim and saw someone standing there at least four hundred feet above him.

The man brought a rifle quickly to his shoulder and fired, the bullet whining off a boulder buried in the gravel beside Longarm. The horse flung up its head at the sound, but Longarm clung to the reins and swiftly mounted up. A second round crashed to the ground in front of the horse. Longarm kept the horse from rearing in panic, clapped his heels to it, and drove it on down the canyon. A huge boulder loomed before him. As he veered around it, a third round smacked off its surface. He kept going, his head bent low over the horse's neck, and saw ahead of him a small bunkhouse huddled close under the canyon wall. He veered toward it, reached it safely, flung himself to the ground, and hauled the horse after him into the bunkhouse.

Inside he found the remains of bunk frames around the walls. The flooring was hard-packed dirt, and early-morning sunlight gleamed through cracks in the roof. Longarm glanced out the doorway. On the canyon rim above, the lone rifleman spilled off his mount, and at the sight of Longarm swung up his rifle and pumped a series of shots methodically through the flimsy shake roof. Longarm pulled the horse after him through the length of the bunkhouse to a second door farther down.

The firing had ceased for a moment. The rifleman was probably busy reloading. The day was already bright and the canyon's shadows fading. He knew that if he stayed where he was a chance shot would sooner or later reach him or cripple his horse. From the pattern of bullet holes on the floor, it was obvious the marksman had set about his job with a design—to cover the bunkhouse from one end to the other—and had covered, so far, at least fifteen feet along the floor.

He peered out the doorway, but his field of vision was too limited for him to see anyone else besides the lone rifleman. As he poked his head out farther, he saw the man dipping his gun's barrel down at him. Longarm ducked back as the rifle detonated, but not before he caught a glimpse of other men riding up to join the rifleman. A second or two later a volley crashed down, smashing through the shake roof and sending clods of dirt flying up from the floor. He caught the reins in his left hand, slapped the horse out through the door, and went up into the saddle. He was twenty feet from the bunkhouse, racing along the narrow meadow paralleling the creek, when the men on the rim swung their fire over and began to reach out for him.

The distance was four hundred feet, and most of the firing was from revolvers, which were not meant for long-range work. But there was some fire from rifles searching him out and coming uncomfortably close. He veered in closer to the cliff wall, occasionally scraping it as he rode, then looked back and up and saw one man leaning out from the rim, trying to land an accurate shot. When it came, the round missed him by three or four yards, exploding the gravel only a few feet ahead of his mount's plunging hooves. He kept going and turned with the cliff's gradual bend, and when he again looked back he found himself sheltered from further fire.

He pulled up to study his position. The canyon made a long, slow turn and opened onto a wide swath of meadowland, while its right-hand wall remained sheer as far as he could see. Across the wide stream rough, thickly timbered shoulders of a ridge were visible. The ridge rose swiftly until it came hard against sheer mountain flanks that lifted almost straight up to a series of jagged peaks.

He left the cover of the canyon wall and galloped full tilt toward the steram. Freshly born in these high hills, the stream was shallow but fast. As the firing came again from behind him, he charged into the water and set the horse upstream for better footing and felt the current break hard against the animal's legs. Longarm kept going, drifting steadily across the stream until, midway across it, the surging water reached as high as the mount's chest. He heard, above the rush of the water, the constant popping sounds of distant rifle fire, and one spent round plunged into the stream alongside him with a faint, gurgling sound. Reaching the far side, the horse struggled to keep its footing on the slippery rocks under its hoofs, came to a full pause to gain its balance, and plunged on again, working through the shallows to dry land.

Just ahead of Longarm across a narrow beach stood the foot of the ridge, a line of timber beginning a few feet farther up the slope. Toward it Longarm urged his mount, and once he gained the shelter of the pines, he stopped and swung around for a look back across the stream.

Matt Forman's men were clearly visible against the side of the cliff, moving down it in single file, following the trail's many switchbacks. He counted eight men, spaced out and moving with great caution as they descended. He thought he recognized Matt Forman's figure, but at that distance he could not be sure. Longarm estimated that in another five minutes the outfit would be at the bottom of the cliff and charging across the stream in hot pursuit.

"So much for being able to keep my head down," Longarm reminded himself ruefully.

He turned his mount and charged up the slope. In about ten minutes he reached a broad upland meadow and charged across it. Once he reached the timber beyond, he dismounted and snaked his Winchester from its boot and slapped his mount's flank, sending it on up the slope ahead of him. He was pretty goddamn sick of running before hot lead, and was looking forward to sending some of his own back at his pursuers. He found a fallen log and made himself comfortable behind it.

As soon as the first rider emerged from the timber, Longarm levered a fresh cartridge into his firing chamber and tracked him. Behind this one, in rapid succession, a hard-driving string of other riders emerged from the timber. Longarm waited to see if the lead rider was Matt Forman, and when it became clear he wasn't, Longarm sighed deeply and let his finger tighten about his trigger. The rifle butt slammed his shoulder, the detonation rolling across the meadow.

The rider yanked suddenly on his mount's reins and lurched backward, dragging the horse violently to one side. The horse stumbled and went to its knees, flinging the rider forward over its neck. The rider struck facedown, rolled over once, then lay still. The other riders coming up from behind spilled to a halt around the downed rider, while two of them flung themselves from their mounts to examine the man.

Longarm turned and raced back up the slope to his horse. Vaulting into the saddle, he kicked the horse on up through the timber. The horse found the footing tough going, but tugged valiantly, doggedly upward over some of the most difficult ground Longarm had ever seen.

At last, as the slope became almost vertical, he found that he had no recourse but to dismount and lead the horse, breaking through vine undergrowth, circling great masses of fallen rock and soil, skirting logs lying breast high before him. The horse came patiently after him, now and then clearing a gully with a lunge that brought the animal hard against Longarm, pushing him sideways and at one time to the ground with awkward, irritating force. It soon became so difficult for the horse to keep its footing on the grade that only Longarm's added weight on the bridle kept the animal from sliding back down the grade.

It went on like this for close to an hour until at last Longarm broke from the timber into a long, grassy plateau. Pulling up wearily, Longarm let his gaze sweep its length. On all sides of the plateau steep peaks reared skyward, and in the distance he saw a short stub of a butte rearing over a low-lying patch of green that extended clear to the horizon.

Longarm had reached the burnout.

Chapter 8

Keeping to the timber, Longarm circled the plateau. When he reached the butte, still screened by a heavy stand of pine, he studied its massive hulk through the trees. How far behind him Matt Forman and his riders were, Longarm had no idea; he had heard no sound of pursuit since reaching the plateau. But they would be showing up soon enough, he had no doubt.

The thing now was to study the burnout, then find a way up onto the butte to wait for Tom Goodnight's arrival.

Still in the timber, he kept moving within the shadow of the butte until he came to a small glen that was little more than a wrinkle in the rough, tangled slope. He rode through it and found himself riding over an area of bald, worn rock, and then was forced to cut around titanic boulders at least two stories high. A moment later, on the other side of the boulders, he broke out of a small stand of alders onto a narrow clearing. There was a stream on the far side, a campfire alight on its bank.

He pulled up at once, looked about him, and saw nothing. But he knew that somewhere on the fringes of this clearing a man stood and held a gun leveled on him. Longarm knew that because of the frying pan beside the fire and the blackened can with hot coffee steaming in it. He dismounted slowly and stood quietly in front of the horse, feeling the danger.

"All right," he said, lifting his head as he looked around. "No need to come out shooting, whoever you are."

He heard a scrape behind him, then the chink of spurs as a boot came down on a solid stretch of caprock. Without a word, a man walked past him with a gun in his hand, swinging it idly at his side. Holstering the gun in a flapped, black-leather Navy holster, he paused by his fire and turned to look at Longarm. The man was in his early forties with a tough, leathery face, thin now with a weariness that seemed bone deep. He pointed to the fire.

"All I got's jerky and some coffee. You're welcome to join me."

"Thanks," Longarm said, turning back to his horse. "I appreciate it."

Working swiftly, Longarm unsaddled his horse, dumped the saddle against the base of a tree, then set the animal loose to crop the fresh green sward at the edge of the clearing. By this time the man had placed the frying pan on the flames and was sitting on a log before it.

"Name's Long," Longarm told the older man as he approached the fire. "Custis Long."

"Jack Tenny. I own the Bar J. Make yourself comfortable."

Longarm sat down on the log beside Tenny. By this time the jerky was sizzling in the frying pan, and Tenny handed Longarm a battered tin cup of black, steaming coffee. Longarm gulped it down noisily, hot as it was. He looked at the jerky in the frying pan and pulled out his pocketknife, helping himself to the meat. Eating alongside him, Tenny chuckled with wry amusement as he recognized Longarm's genuine hunger.

"That horse of yours looked plumb tuckered out. Man shouldn't drive a mount into the ground like that."

"I had no choice," Longarm told him, using the last of his coffee to wash down the jerky.

"You got fellers on your tail?"

"Matt Forman and his riders."

"That so?" he said, glancing sidelong at Longarm. "Eat up then, and welcome."

Longarm thanked the man and poured himself another cup of coffee from the pot sitting in the coals. Then, his hunger satisfied, he leaned back, took out a cheroot for himself, and handed one to Tenny. After they had both lit up, Longarm glanced more closely at Tenny and became aware of something familiar in his face, an echo of someone else.

Tenny saw the look on Longarm's face. "I guess you see my father in my face."

"Your father?"

"Abe Tenny. He worked at the Sun Ranch. Something about loyalty to Buckman and that daughter of his."

"I was there, Tenny. I'm sorry about what happened."

"In Placer Town, Ellen told me it was you pulled my father out of their burning ranch house."

"He'd been shot up bad. I don't think he felt the flames."

"I know what killed him, Long. A bullet sent by Matt Forman or one of his hired killers. I blame myself," Tenny went on. "I rode in that night to warn Sun Ranch. If I hadn't, their crew wouldn't have turned tail."

At once Longarm recalled the beat of hooves deep in the timber below him that night; this was the rider he had followed, the one who had, in a sense, been the reason he had reached the blazing ranch house when he had.

"I heard you that night. It was your hoofbeats I followed to the Sun Ranch. Tell me, after you warned Buckman, why did you ride out?"

His glance was miserable. "Damn it, Long. I had the Bar J to think about, and a wife and boy to get to safety in Placer Town. Forman knew by that time I wouldn't go along with him anymore, that I was willing to throw in with Buckman. And he wouldn't have that. When the dust clears, he aims to be the biggest cattleman in this territory."

"Why's he so anxious for that?"

Tenny grinned thinly. "I believe there's a woman involved."

"Kate Summerfield?"

"Matt is determined to marry her, and to do that he figures he has to impress her. He thinks this is the way."

"He might have Kate all wrong."

"He might, and then again, he might not. But that don't matter much, one way or the other. What matters is that Matt Forman thinks he has to do this."

"What are you doing here, Tenny?"

"I want Matt Forman's head for the killing of my father."

"I want Matt too."

"Ellen told me it was Gil you was after."

"You haven't heard then. Gil is dead. So is Clem Jagger."

"No, I hadn't heard. But now that I think of it, I haven't seen Jagger or Gil lately."

"There's something else you should know. I'm expecting a posse tonight. We're going into the burnout after the cattle."

"Are you now? And where are you going to get this posse?"

"Tom Goodnight's bringing his riders and as many other cattlemen as he can gather."

Tenny rubbed his stubbled jaw reflectively. It sounded like a file on sandpaper. "Well, there won't be all that many. I can tell you that, Long. Matt has them fellers worn to a nubbin'. They don't have the sand for any direct action, and Matt knows it."

"You mean that's what he's been counting on."

"They haven't stopped him yet."

"Well, then, how do you plan to stop him, Tenny?"

He chuckled, lifted the pan off the fire and slapped it a couple of times with the side of his tin cup. Longarm saw a man step out of the brush across the clearing. He heard movement to his right, and glancing in that direction saw two more armed men stepping into view. Four more men left the timber surrounding the small clearing and walked toward them.

"This is how, Long," Tenny said. "These are men who worked for the other hill ranchers until they found themselves competing with Forman's hired gunslicks."

"I count seven men," Longarm replied. "You think that's enough to stop Matt Forman?"

"Well now, if Tom Goodnight comes through like you think he will, it just might be. Besides, all I really want is a clear shot at that son of a bitch, Matt Forman."

Tossing the butt of his cheroot to one side, he stood up and led Longarm through the timber, his men following. They emerged from the timber close under the butte, and Tenny headed for a narrow game trail that wound up its side. The climb was steep, and when they reached the top, Longarm saw two men crouched behind two fat boulders on the rim.

As Tenny conferred with his lookouts, Longarm walked to the far side of the butte and watched as great, anvil-topped thunderheads spilled high into the sky beyond the peaks. In the dark caverns below them, lightning flickered like the tongues of snakes. The sky itself had become like a flat, slate-colored sheet. Watching the storm clouds and feeling the oppressive, muggy closeness in the air, Longarm realized that before this night was over, rain was almost a certainty.

He looked down at the burnout. He was suitably impressed by its extent, and also by its seeming impenetrability. If those rustled cattle were still in there, there was sure as hell no sign of them, and Longarm began to grasp why it was that Tom Goodnight and his fellow cattlemen seemed so helpless before Matt Forman's depredations.

Tenny approached him.

"Matt Forman and seven other riders came up a little while ago and disappeared into the burnout." He looked closely at Longarm. "One of them was in a bad way."

"We did exchange shots, and that's a fact."

"Then it looks like you might have evened the odds a mite. I tell you what, Long. I say we don't wait for Goodnight. I say we go in right now, while it's still daylight."

"I heard that was a tough place to get out of, let alone get into."

"And how did you and Goodnight expect to do it?"

"We were going to replace the men Matt leaves behind along the route he takes into the place."

Tenny considered that. "Not a bad idea," he said, approvingly. "But there's a good chance that could go haywire, and you'd need a lot of men."

"That's what Goodnight is promising. Like I said, a posse."

"You ever hear of the Minotaur, Long?"

"It's a Greek myth."

"A girl gave this fellow a sword so he could enter a maze and kill the Minotaur, and also a thread to follow out of the maze."

"You mean you have such a thread?"

He grinned. "Not thread, just a lot of good, strong fishing tackle."

"Fishing tackle?"

"You heard right."

Longarm grinned suddenly, realizing what Tenny was suggesting. He liked it. "How much do you have?"

"Enough to reach from here to Salt Lake City."

"You think you'll need that much?"

"You'll find out when you get inside that burnout."

Longarm glanced at the sky. The encroaching storm clouds had not yet blotted out the sun, which was still high enough to keep portions of the sky bright, but shadows cast by the surrounding peaks were already reaching across the plateau. If they were going to go in after Matt Forman, they would have to make their move soon.

"Okay," he said to Tenny. "Let's go."

"I'll leave these two men up here to watch for Goodnight."

Longarm agreed and descended the butte with Tenny and his men.

An hour later, following a well-worn path through the green tangle of underbrush, they came to a fork in the trail. Longarm and Tenny were in the lead, the rest of Tenny's men strung out behind them.

"Which way?" Longarm asked.

Tenny pointed to the ground near a clump of junipers. Barely visible along the ground was a gleaming thread that vanished ahead of them into the right-hand trail.

"How'd that get there?" Longarm asked him.

"We've been damn busy the last couple of nights."

Longarm looked about him, a puzzled frown on his face. "I haven't seen any sign of those men Goodnight said Forman stationed at strategic turnings."

"Hell, Long. I figure he don't bother with that no more. He's been getting his own way for so long he figures he's damn near impregnable inside the burnout. And up until now, he ain't been far wrong."

"Well, then. Let's see what we can do to change that."

Following the thread, they broke out at length into a marshy area. The trail ahead of them now became pocked with hoof marks, and there were places where it was obvious some cattle had become bogged. They caught the tracks left by struggling horses, and in more than a few places they saw where men's boots had been sucked deep into the marshy ground as the men struggled to free the bogged cattle.

Once beyond the marshy area, they found themselves in rolling country covered with fir and juniper growth little more than five or six feet high, with a nearly impenetrable natural barrier of wild grapevines and other creepers woven densely in among them. Topping a slight rise, they came upon four different game trails branching off through the solid growth. Here the ground was hard-packed, very little vegetation covering it, with patches of volcanic caprock showing through.

The four breaks in the hedgelike growth opened onto trails that could take them in four different directions, and by this time, the vines and juniper had given way to a murderous tangle of broomstick-thick alders and punishing brush that tore cruelly at a rider's unprotected thighs.

Pulling up on the ridge, Longarm glanced at Tenny.

"Looks like this is as far as you go with that thread of yours."

Tenny nodded. "True. But I got plenty more line to put down."

He motioned to four of his riders, who pulled up promptly alongside him. Tenny handed each a thick roll of tackle. The men rode to the breaks in the alder brush at the head of each trail, tied the thin lines to the bases of bushes, then mounted up and followed the separate trails until they vanished into the burnout, trailing the thread behind them.

Dismounting, Tenny led his horse off the ridge, the rest of his men following his example.

"Now we wait," Tenny told Longarm.

A still, moonless darkness had fallen by the time three of Tenny's four men returned, each one confessing failure. That left the fourth man, and when he did not return, Tenny told his men to mount up. Then he walked over to the remaining trail, and letting the line the missing rider had laid down run lightly through his gloved fingers, he stepped into his saddle and rode at the head of his men still deeper into the burnout.

The night had become oppressively sultry, the thunderheads that Longarm had observed earlier now directly overhead. Dim peals of thunder had been grumbling in the distance, and lightning flashes as swift as thought now winked in among the encircling peaks. It was only a matter of time before the sky over their heads opened up.

Yet even in the inky darkness Longarm was able to see the backs of at least four hundred head of cattle ahead of him. They were bedded down for the night on a large, open flat that was cut by a broad, black ribbon of a stream. Astride his horse, Longarm shook his head and shucked his hat back off his forehead. Not until that moment had it dawned on him just how massive was the hemorrhage Matt Forman's rustling had been inflicting on Goodnight's herds, or on those of the other cattlemen.

Dismounting, and with Tenny and Longarm in the lead, they led their horses around the rim of the herd, heading for a campfire all of them could now see pulsing dimly on the far side. They were halfway to it when they came upon the body of the rider Tenny had sent ahead of them. In one hand he was clutching the remnants of the line he had been trailing, in the other his Colt.

Tenny swore bitterly as Longarm went down on one knee alongside the man and lifted the Colt's muzzle to his nostril. It had not been fired. Handing the gun up to Tenny, he stood up himself and looked quickly around. The dead man had been left there deliberately, as a marker as well as a warning. It meant only one thing. They were now expected.

"Forget that fire," Longarm told Tenny. "That's just a decoy."

Tenny nodded nervously, and the men crowding around them began looking in every direction.

"Over there!" someone muttered, pointing.

Looking, they saw the heads and shoulders of mounted men pushing through the herd directly toward them, while other riders were approaching from around the edges of the herd.

"Damn it," Tenny muttered. "We walked right into

142

this one. We better get back into the brush." As he spoke, he unlimbered his Colt and cocked the hammer.

"Think again," counseled Longarm quietly. "If we retreat now, they'll just cut us down at their leisure, like shooting rabbits, or they'll just keep us in the burnout until we starve."

"You got any ideas, Long?"

"I say we mount up and stampede that herd back over them, then keep the herd going until we're out of this. I can't think of a better way to make a new trail out of this tangle than with a stampeding herd."

Tenny grinned. "We'll do it."

He told his men what to do and mounted up. Nodding grimly, the men mounted up also and drew their weapons. Tenny raised his six-gun and punched a hole in the sky. A ragged chorus of gunfire backed him, and as the sudden detonations thundered across the herd, the cattle leapt to their feet like one single, massive animal, and turning about, stampeded away from the gunfire, the ground trembling under their hooves.

Keeping after the maddened animals, Longarm sent his own shots into the air over the plunging sea of backs as Tenny's men spread out in a long line on both sides of him. The herd was in full, frantic flight now, plunging through the sultry darkness in a reasonably straight course with no sound of clicking horns, only the soul-chilling thunder of their pounding hooves. There was nothing now that was going to turn this herd.

Ahead of him he caught the flash of gunfire as Forman's men tried to turn or split the herd. Their efforts were futile, but they managed to crowd the herd's leaders, and now Longarm heard the sound of clicking horns as the cattle came together. Longarm saw some of the cattle, crazed with fear, milling frantically, their heads jammed, their horns locked, a few rearing up and riding over others, the mass of them squirming like bristling snakes.

By this time most of Forman's riders were completely caught up in the torrent of cattle. Some of them were trying to outrun the cattle, while others, overtaken or caught in the cattle's midst, struggled to keep in their saddles. They were shooting wildly about them in a desperate effort to force a way out of this headlong stream, their gun flashes illuminating their desperate faces. Their struggle did not last long as, with grim finality, horses and riders were caught up in the relentless tide and trampled under.

At that moment Longarm's own horse plunged over the lip of a steep gully. His horse lit heavily, stumbled forward, and went to its knees. Hauling it back up onto its feet, Longarm booted the horse up the far bank of the gully. Once more in sight of the herd, Longarm saw that it had narrowed into a massive stream funneling back through the burnout. Though he could not be absolutely certain in the darkness, it seemed to him that the stampeding cattle were not making a new path out of the burnout. They were simply—and sensibly—fleeing from the burnout over the same path they had taken to get in.

Meanwhile, Tenny's men had come upon those of Matt Forman's gunslicks who had managed to survive the stampede. Lead filled the air as they flung shots at each other. But in the stygian darkness, few of the men could have been very certain who they were shooting at.

144

There was great confusion and yelling, horses whinnied in terror as they were struck by bullets or dragged to the ground by wounded riders. Gun flashes lit the night eerily. Then, with unnerving suddenness, as if anxious to put in its two cents, the cloudburst that had been gathering crashed full upon them.

The storm's sudden violence stunned Longarm with its fearful impact. Thunder rent the air with a palpable force that almost drove him off his horse. Lightning flickered and flashed constantly, playing a hideous blue light over the burnout and the plunging backs of the stampeding cattle. And with it, just as suddenly, came a downpour that was nothing less than a mean, persistent assault on him and his horse and any creature caught under its furious lash.

He rode on nevertheless, with Tenny and his men driving the cattle before them on a beeline straight out of the burnout. The animals went with a will, plunging before the terrible, winking fingers of light and the numbing cracks of thunder. Before long he passed the marshy spot they had come upon when entering the place and found it deep in swirling water. It should have slowed the cattle some, but they did not hesitate as they charged on blindly through the night, driven as much by the awesome cloudburst close over their heads as by the horsemen chasing after them.

Longarm was not entirely aware when it was they had managed to put the burnout behind them. At any rate, the going—for him and the cattle, at least—was considerably easier as they continued on across the high plateau. Ahead of him, through the slanting curtains of rain lit by continuous flashes of lightning, he made out some of Tenny's riders, and beyond them, the surging cattle.

Then he saw Tenny. The man was racing after one of Forman's riders from the looks of it. His revolver was out and he was sending fire after the fleeing horseman. Digging his heels into his mount's flanks, Longarm urged it after Tenny. As he was about to overtake Tenny from his left side, Longarm caught sight of another hostile rider coming at Tenny from his blind side. Abruptly, in an effort to head off this rider, Longarm cut toward him. But the sudden change in direction was too much for his overworked horse. The animal lost its footing on the mud-slicked ground and Longarm felt it go down under him, flinging him forward over its neck.

He somersaulted in midair, his back striking the ground with numbing force, then spun wickedly through the mud. He was still holding his Colt, but felt his grip slacken. And then a boulder embedded in the ground caught him on the side of the head, and Longarm exploded into darkness.

It was still raining. The heavy drops were pounding down on his back as he lay sprawled facedown beside the boulder. He felt as if every bone in his body had been fractured, but when he tried to move his limbs, he found they still responded, though not without protest. He was about to push himself off the ground when he heard two horsemen riding up through the rain toward him. He recognized their voices instantly and froze. One of them was Matt Forman.

And the other was Tom Goodnight.

"I still say it was your fault," Forman told Goodnight angrily.

"How the hell was I to know Tenny and his men were already out here?" Goodnight replied, just as angry. "I sent Long to the butte figuring he'd be alone."

"Well, it's done now," Matt groused, his voice heavy with mean desperation. "I lost more than half my men."

"Maybe you better keep your ass down until this blows over. It don't look like Tenny's going to be an easy man to stop."

"I don't care how it looks, Goodnight. If you ain't got the guts for this, just say so. But I'm going to keep the pressure on them fool cattlemen or they'll never sell out."

"Okay, okay," Goodnight told him. "Suit yourself."

Tom Goodnight was no match for Matt Forman—and apparently never had been. That show he had put on when he took Longarm's side and turned back Matt and his brother Gil had been just that. A show. One he had put on for his men. It would not do for them to know he had thrown in with Matt Forman.

Longarm heard the saddle squeak as Goodnight leaned over to study Longarm's still figure. "What're we goin' to do about this federal marshal?"

"He looks dead enough to me."

"He's a tough one. You sure he's dead?"

Forman nudged his horse closer, dismounted, and kicked Longarm over onto his back. Longarm kept his eyes closed, his face slack. There was a pause while Forman studied Longarm's face.

"Maybe you're right. Let's get out of here."

Only when Longarm heard the dim mutter of fading hoofbeats did he release his hold on consciousness and slip back into the void.

It was daylight when he awoke a second time. The rain was still pounding his head and shoulders. Inside his head the pounding rain was magnified, his teeth were chattering, and his sodden clothing weighed a ton. But that steady freshet of blood was no longer pouring from his nostril.

Gingerly he felt his aching head, and marveled at the fact that he was still alive. This was not the first time death's messenger had brushed him this closely, and it would probably not be the last. He just hoped he didn't make a habit of it. He thought he could make out the dim, massive outline of the butte on the far side of the flat. He was sore and whatever hinges and bolts held him together were sure as hell loosened up some. And nothing, it seemed, could banish the steady pounding in his head.

He started walking, his eyes peering intently through the rain at the ground, looking for sign. Soon enough he came upon the trail left by the stampeding cattle, but already the rain was washing out most of their tracks. He kept walking, saw a horse on its side thrashing feebly, and detoured toward it. Pulling his derringer out of the side pocket where it had rested since he took it back from Brothers, he killed the horse and kept on.

Almost across the plateau, close in under the butte, he pulled up suddenly. Less than twenty yards from him his horse was standing with its head drooping. Calling

148

softly to it, he approached cautiously. The animal's ears flickered hopefully and it nickered at the sight of him. Longarm called out a second time, hoping his familiar voice would remind the horse of that long climb they had made through the darkness the night before. And that seemed to do it. Though the animal watched him warily, it allowed Longarm to grab the reins and pull it closer.

Fitting his boot into the stirrup, he hauled his right leg over the cantle and straightened up in the saddle. The universe rocked drunkenly around his head for a moment, and he waited for it to settle back into its usual orbit before hauling the horse around. Then he rode back toward the burnout, his eyes searching the ground, hoping against hope to find his .44. He had just left the burnout, he remembered, when he had veered sharply over to help Tenny.

His luck now turned. Through the rain he saw the gleam of his six-gun's cylinder and barrel, its grips almost entirely buried in the mud. And sitting on the ground beside it was his hat, crown up. He dismounted, picked up the weapon and examined it. It would need to be cleaned entirely, but at least he still had it. He dropped his revolver into his cross-draw rig and plucked his hat out of the mud. Cleaning off the sweatband with his forefinger, he put it on, ignoring his aching head and the gash in his skull.

Hauling his creaking limbs back into his saddle, he wondered what time it was and glanced up through the steady rain. He thought he could see the sun's placement, which meant it was now late afternoon of the next day. Plenty of time had elapsed since they stampeded that herd out of the burnout.

And from what he had overheard later, Tom Goodnight was playing a lone hand, with none of his riders —and certainly not Ellen Buckman—aware of his link with Matt. His motivation was clear enough to Longarm: With the other cattlemen driven off, there would be plenty of land left to be divided evenly between Goodnight and Forman—and no one the wiser. And it would not surprise Longarm to learn that Goodnight was getting a share of the profits gained from the sale of all that rustled beef.

And when it was all over, Ellen Buckman would end up married to the man who had been in league with her father's killer.

Chapter 9

The rain let up, and close to nightfall Longarm came
upon a homesteader's cabin high in the range on the
edge of a narrow belt of stream-fed meadowland. The
soil here, Longarm could not help noting, was thin, the
grass precariously rooted; and at this altitude, not only
was the growing season short, but the winters must have
been brutal. All this the homesteader's place reflected.

The log cabin was ringed with piñon stumps. Its roof
was of sod squares and its ridgepole sagged. The privy
sat crookedly behind the cabin on an uneven hole dug
half-heartedly from the stony soil. Filling the front yard
was a litter of rusted farm implements, a rotting mat-
tress, a wheelless buggy, and an overturned grindstone.
Only the pole barn seemed to be the result of a solid
effort on the homesteader's part.

A few chickens feeding in the front yard scattered,

clucking indignantly at Longarm's approach, and a ragged-looking collie left the barn to bark at him. The combined racket brought the homesteader out of the cabin. He was carrying a Hawken. A sharp rebuke caused the collie to slink miserably back into the barn. Behind the homesteader came his wife, a large, swollen, lank-haired creature. The rotting porch sagged dangerously under her.

Longarm pulled up his horse and waited for the homesteader to lower his Hawken. When he did, Longarm nodded to the woman lurking behind her husband. "Howdy, ma'am."

She muttered something to her husband, scratched the back of her head, then turned and vanished back into the house.

"I'm looking for the Lazy M," Longarm told the homesteader.

The fellow regarded Longarm sourly. His sunken cheeks and cadaverous frame bore mute testimony to his lack of success in this desolate farming region. His examination of Longarm complete, he expectorated a black gob of chewing tobacco at a plant poking up beside his porch. "You got a ways to go yet, mister. But you're welcome to light and set a spell. There's plenty of water and oats for your hoss. And for supper we got some potatoes and roots, if you've a mind to join us."

Longarm nodded. It was a poor sort of man who turned down any offer of hospitality. "My thanks," he told the homesteader.

"See to your hoss then. I'll tell my woman to set another place at the table." He turned and went back inside.

Longarm swung stiffly out of his saddle and led his horse into the barn. Though the rain had stopped hours before, he had ridden through a gray, sunless world, and the dampness had seeped deep into his bones. He hoped there would be a wood fire inside.

There was no wood fire, and the one-room interior of the cabin was dank and gloomy, lighted by a single coal-oil lamp hung from a rafter. It took an anxious moment or two for Longarm to accustom his stomach to the cabin's stench. It was compounded of coal oil, unwashed bodies, and swill—all concentrated, it seemed, into a fetid cloud that hung like a curse over the table.

The roots the homesteader had mentioned turned out to be turnips. Together with the potatoes simmering in a thick, meaty broth, they made for a supper hearty enough to warm Longarm's insides clear down to his boot heels. He made it a point not to ask what kind of meat was in the stew.

The meal finished, the homesteader—whose name was Frank Stanton—reached under the table for a jug of corn liquor and passed it across to Longarm. As Longarm lifted the jug to his mouth, the liquor's smell reminded him of a mildewed silo. A moment later, as he wiped off his mouth and blinked the tears from his eyes, he wondered if he hadn't just swallowed a lighted kerosene lamp.

Longarm handed the jug back to Stanton. The man lifted it high, swallowed twice, then handed the jug over to his wife. Milly was her name, and she had been waiting eagerly. She snatched the jug and took two long swallows, wiped her lips, then took two more.

Longarm saw the alarm on Stanton's face. "Milly,

you hold up some," he snapped. "Don't take advantage of the fact we got ourselves a guest here."

Reluctantly Milly handed the jug back to her husband. He took a quick swig, then placed the jug down on the table between him and Longarm.

"You're on your way to Matt Forman's spread," he said. "That right?"

Longarm nodded.

"You one of his hired gunslicks from Silver Creek?"

"No, I am not."

"What's your business with Forman?"

"It's personal, Stanton."

"He a friend of yours, is he?"

"No."

"Well, he's no friend of mine, either. All that beef he's rustlin', and the son of a bitch resents it when I liberate one or two scraggly head to feed my family."

"What's the best trail to the Lazy M?"

"Tell him, Frank," said his wife.

Stanton shrugged. "Just keep on over the ridge the way you was going. You'll dip into a valley. Go east then over a ridge for at least a couple of hours until you come to a long flat and you'll see the Lazy M ranch buildings."

"How long a ride is it?"

"Half a day's ride, maybe."

"Guess I'll get a move on, then."

Stanton reached for the jug and handed it to Longarm. "Take another bite of this," he urged.

Longarm took the bottle and let the moonshine explode down his gullet. Then, seeing the pleading light in Milly Stanton's eyes, he handed the jug to her. She took it eagerly and managed two quick swallows before her husband snatched the jug from her.

Longarm got to his feet.

Stanton looked at his wife. "We got room for Long to stay the night, Milly?"

"Why, sure," she replied. Then she looked at Longarm. "Mr. Long, you don't need to ride out tonight. You kin sleep in the barn."

"I'd appreciate that," Longarm told her.

He leapt at the prospect of escaping the confines of this grim cabin. The good, clean, honest smell of fresh horse manure and urine stomped into old hay would be a welcome relief. He thanked the woman for his supper and bid the two of them good night.

A moment later, crossing the littered yard outside, he sucked in the high, clear mountain air with enormous relief.

Longarm's sleep was fitful and restless, punctuated with nightmares of plunging cattle and gun flashes. At one point he abruptly sat up, fully awake in an instant. A knife blade in Frank Stanton's upraised hand glinted in the darkness above him. Longarm rolled swiftly to one side as the blade plunged down, the force of its thrust sinking the tip deep into the rotting floorboard. Longarm grabbed Stanton's wrist and twisted. The homesteader cried out and released his hold on the knife. Longarm jumped to his feet and hauled Stanton up after him.

Letting go of Stanton's wrist, Longarm punched the man in his midsection, reaching deep enough to crack the man's backbone. Uttering a small cry as the wind was knocked out of him, Stanton slammed back against the side of a stall. Longarm kept after him remorselessly, punching him in the face twice, each blow a powerful, measured stroke. Stanton's head snapped back, this time striking against one of the barn's poles. Longarm bore in without mercy, punching him in the face and then in the belly, as deep or deeper than the first time. Gasping, Stanton doubled over. Longarm stood back then and caught him with a well-timed uppercut that caught him flush on the jaw and sent his head flying up, the rear of it crunching into the pole again, this time with sickening force.

Uttering a deep, discouraged sigh, Frank Stanton slid down the length of the pole, collapsing forward at last into a pile of horse manure. Longarm grabbed the man's lank hair and lifted his head. In the dim light he could see blood trickling from his right nostril. As Longarm held him, Stanton's eyes opened and he groaned softly.

Longarm heard cautious steps crossing the yard. He let Stanton's head fell forward again and ducked below the stall's side as Milly Stanton stepped cautiously into the barn's open doorway. She was having trouble seeing into the barn's black gloom. She was carrying her husband's Hawken. Swiftly Longarm groped in the hay for the knife Stanton had dropped. He found it and held it up. From what little light filtered into the barn, he could see it was a buffalo knife, its long blade honed to a nasty cutting edge. By this time Stanton's wife had taken an uncertain step into the barn and was peering nervously about her.

Longarm grabbed Stanton's hair and placed the knife against his neck, letting its sharp edge break the skin.

He felt Stanton come awake and pull back, gasping.

"I got Frank's knife," Longarm called to Milly. "And I'm holding it against his neck. Drop the rifle or I'll slit his throat."

She promptly bent and laid the rifle down. "I told him you was an Indian and could see in the dark," she said resignedly.

Longarm left Frank and picked up the rifle. "Frank's back in there," he told her. "You better see to him. He's had a nasty crack on the head."

She hurried past him and left the barn a moment later with her cadaverous husband in her arms, carrying him as easily as a child would a rag doll.

She spent most of the night swabbing her husband's head, taking time out at dawn to make herself and Longarm an enormous breakfast of steak and eggs and fried potatoes, which Longarm consumed on the porch. As Longarm mounted up afterward, she stepped off the porch and walked over to peer up at him.

"No hard feelin's, mister?" she said, shading her eyes. "Frank never did have much sense about these matters. He saw you in Placer Town when Matt's men was after you, and he just figured he could make a trade with Matt—your body for some beef cattle. We're runnin' low."

"He's lucky I didn't kill him," was all Longarm said. She stepped back and he rode out.

Some distance from the cabin Longarm glanced back. Milly Stanton was sitting on the porch in a rocker, holding the jug of moonshine in her lap and singing hymns in a high, quavering voice, praising the Lord for her deliverance. Longarm was not sure whether it was deliverance from him or from the vigilance of her husband, who had kept her so long from the jug.

He turned back around and kept going on his way to Matt Forman's Lazy M.

Just as Kate Summerfield had told him, the Lazy M ranch buildings sat on a flat at the end of a long, lush pasture that reached for miles, clear to a high pass in the distance. Despite the fine quality of the pasture, as Longarm rode across it, he saw no sign of Lazy M cattle. Indeed, during the long ride down the center of the rolling pastureland, he managed to spook only a few jackrabbits. Within a half mile of the ranch buildings, Longarm moved into the timber bordering the flat and kept up the slope until he found a clear ridge above the ranch. He dismounted in the timber in back of the ridge, walked to the other side of it, found a tree and slumped down, his back to it. Then he lit a cheroot, his Winchester resting across his knees.

It was midafternoon and so quiet below that for a dismal while Longarm considered the possibility that he had arrived at an empty ranch, that Matt Forman and most of his riders were possibly in Silver Creek licking their wounds. Or else he and his men had ridden into Placer Town.

And then the door opened in the small bunkhouse just below him and out onto the low porch stepped Frank Tyson, the rider who had followed Longarm from Sheridan City. Matt Forman stepped out after him and pulled the door shut. As the two men stepped off the porch, Longarm raised his rifle, sighted, and fired.

Longarm saw the spurt of dust kick up in front of Tyson. Without looking, the man flung himself back onto the porch. Matt spun to look up at Longarm, a six-gun materializing in his hand. At that distance, Longarm realized, Matt could not make out who he was. But Matt obviously saw the glint of his rifle barrel and flung himself after Tyson onto the porch. Longarm put two quick shots into the side of the bunkhouse as the two men disappeared inside.

Longarm bellied down beside the tree, put his sights on the door, and sent two slugs through it. He saw the wood leaping as the lead punched through, the smack of each slug coming on the heels of his rifle's report. He waited a moment, then put two shots through the window. He moved his sights and put another shot into the door, and then levered fresh shells into the Winchester, watching.

The faint shout of angry, confused voices in the bunkhouse came to him. Suddenly there was a shot, and Longarm heard the thud of the bullet in the tree above him. He smiled a little and moved deeper behind the tree trunk, and then put two more shots through the window. He heard a bitter cursing inside the bunkhouse, settled himself comfortably onto the grass, and waited. Presently a barrel poked out of the bunkhouse's shattered window, and Longarm quickly put a shot at it. The barrel withdrew. Longarm put three quick shots into the door and then, on a whim, raised his sights to the stovepipe. It took four shots to bring it down. The pipe bent, broke, rolled down the sod roof, and boomed twice as it hit the ground and rolled to a stop.

Again Longarm loaded his Winchester, and this time he put the rifle aside, waiting.

Nothing moved below him. Neither Forman nor Tyson offered to come out and settle this like reasonable men. But this did not disappoint or surprise Longarm. He had no warrant for Matt Forman's arrest, and Longarm was convinced by now that it was Matt Forman— not his brother Gil—who had killed Aleta Crowley. Yet there was no way Longarm could bring Matt in legally, and even if he did manage that, Longarm believed that no jury in the world would convict Matt Forman of either crime.

On the other hand, if Matt Forman came at Longarm like a wet hornet, and Longarm was forced to kill him in self-defense, a crude but effective justice would finally prevail. Longarm was now in the act of pouring water on a hornet's nest.

Abruptly a rifle opened up on Longarm from a rise beyond the ranch house. There was a third man down there after all. He must have been in the ranch house when Longarm opened up. The rifleman's fire was rapid and not very accurate, but Longarm could not afford to ignore it. As he picked up his rifle and ducked back into the trees, he saw Forman and Tyson bolt from the bunkhouse, heading for the barn.

Longarm reached his horse, cinched the saddle tight, and vaulted into it. He headed up the timbered slope, skirting behind the ranch buildings, and kept to its cover for a mile until he regained the flat. He was a good two miles across the flat, heading south, when he glanced behind him and saw the first horseman boil out of the timber in pursuit, and behind him came two others. That first horseman, Longarm knew, would be Matt Forman. Slowing down some, he peered more closely at the other two and saw that the third rider—the rifleman who had opened up on him from behind the ranch house—was Bull Bronson, the big logger who had worked Seth Barton over on the night Longarm rode into Placer Town.

He waited a moment to make sure the hook was in all the way, then clapped his heels to his mount and resumed his flight, swinging to the southwest into a patch of timber, pleased. There were still long hours of daylight and miles of open country before him. Matt Forman and his two gunslicks would be furious enough to push their mounts ruthlessly, but not wisely.

Longarm now had his way. On his tail were three angry wet hornets.

The mouth of the canyon looked about right, and as Longarm splashed across the broad, shallow stream, he realized he had passed this way before, had dimly remembered it as he rode, and had deliberately headed toward it.

Dismounting, he slapped his horse's rump smartly, sending it toward a grassy sward, partially shielded by a break in the canyon wall. Then he flattened himself behind a low pile of rocks beside the stream and waited. His pursuers would soon be charging after him into the canyon's mouth in plain sight, and there would be nothing but an open stream between them.

Before long, he heard the pounding hooves approaching the canyon. Longarm placed his Colt on the ground beside him. The three riders appeared, racing after him recklessly, certain their numbers would be sufficient to take him.

Longarm tracked the nearest rider, the big logger, and squeezed the trigger. His horse dropped under him, spilling him forward onto the ground. Matt and Tyson reined in and pulled their mounts around so frantically they nearly went down. Longarm levered quickly, tracked Matt Forman, and fired. The shot missed and a second later the two riders were out of sight.

Longarm ran out from cover and splashed across the broad stream. Skirting the dead horse, Longarm saw Bull Bronson push himself up onto his hands and knees. His hat lay beside him.

"Get up, Bull," Longarm told him.

Fear and anger were in Bull's eyes. He pushed himself upright. "I ain't got nothin' against you, mister."

"You didn't have anything against Seth Barton either, but that didn't stop you from setting him up."

"I did what I was told."

"By your keeper. By Matt Forman."

Puzzled, Bull twisted his head to peer at Longarm more closely. "This here is crazy. Matt said he killed you."

"Matt shouldn't brag like that."

Bull shook his head and peered intently at Longarm, obviously feeling a lot better. The fall off his horse had stunned him only momentarily. "You better get out of here, mister," he told Longarm evenly. "Matt's goin' to be back here soon. This time he won't miss."

"Drop your gun belt."

"Sure. I don't need this."

Bull's hands dropped to the buckle, then paused. The

162

big logger's eyes narrowed. Then Longarm saw the muscles of his right shoulder jerk suddenly as he reached back for his gun butt.

Almost reluctantly, Longarm flipped up his rifle and squeezed the trigger. But Bull's gun swept up with startling speed and rapped sharply against the barrel of Longarm's rifle, brushing it aside. Longarm's shot went wild. He ducked. Bill fired at him hastily. The shot seared past Longarm's shoulder, its passage a hot whisper in his left ear. Down on one knee, Longarm brought up his rifle, caught Bull's immense chest in his sight and fired again.

The sound of his rifle was the only thing he heard. He saw Bull's body jerk and the big man fought to stay on his feet, dropped to his knees, then pitched heavily forward onto his face. Where his chest struck the soft, gravelly soil, a dark stain welled into view.

Longarm walked over to Bull and stood above him, aware of his own heart pounding, and of the still-heightened awareness of himself and the world about him. He was about to reach down for Bull's six-gun when he heard behind him a sound he recognized immediately—a Winchester's lever jacking in a fresh cartridge.

Without looking, Longarm turned and raced back across the stream. The rifle cracked and a bullet sent a geyser of water into the air inches from his plunging left foot. Reaching the other side of the stream, he half crawled, half dived for the shelter of the rocks, and hit the ground with a violence that jarred him to his bones.

He flattened himself behind the rocks and swung up his rifle, his eye on the other side of the stream. Above the rim of a depression he saw the rifleman's hat outlined and then a rifle barrel. Longarm steadied his weapon, sighted carefully, and squeezed off a shot. The hat jumped and vanished, but the rifle remained steady. Its muzzle blazed. Before its echo died, a bullet whanged angrily off the rock beside him.

Longarm waited a while without returning fire, and when a second shot came from the same source, he realized that another man was circling around to get him from the rear. Longarm was not surprised. It was what he would have done in a similar situation. He put his rifle aside and drew his .44, waiting for another shot from across the stream. When it came, the slug whining off a rock in front of him, he leapt to his feet and ran out from the rocks, heading back toward the canyon wall.

As he ran, he saw a stalking figure on the rim above him. Frank Tyson. Longarm saw Tyson's rifle come to his shoulder, then saw the flash. The ground at his feet exploded, sending tiny shards of rock up into his face. He ducked his face away, reached a cleft in the cliff wall and, running into it, saw a narrow game trail, the same one that Matt Forman and his riders had moved down when pursuing him earlier. He charged up the trail, Tyson no longer visible on the rim. From the canyon below him, Matt Forman, standing in plain sight on the other side of the stream, sent a hail of lead at him, but the distance was too great, the bullets no more than a distant whine when they struck.

Approaching the rim, Longarm did not check his stride, only bent his body a little. Then, his legs driving him steadily up the steep trail, he dove onto his belly over the rim, his Colt out ahead of him.

The blast of Frank Tyson's rifle was almost in his face. He was blinded by its flash and the sting of the gravel thrown up by the bullet, and landed heavily on his belly. He shot blindly then, emptying his gun with closed eyes, cursing doggedly and furiously. Nothing answered him. He lay still a bare second, blinking the hot, smarting tears out of his eyes, and slowly, as if seen through deep water, the sprawled body of Frank Tyson lying on his face not six feet away became clear to him.

He pushed himself erect and heard, coming from the floor of the canyon below him, the sudden rapid beat of hooves. He ran over to the rim and was in time to glimpse Matt Forman's back as he vanished down the canyon, heading south for Placer Town.

Chapter 10

Longarm rode into Placer Town late that night. He reckoned that Matt Forman was at least an hour ahead of him, but as he clopped down the main street, he saw no sign of the man, or of anyone else, for that matter. The only light came from the window in the doc's office, but the saloons were dark, despite the horses lined up at the hitch racks in front of them, and the light on the hotel porch was out. Furthermore, no light came from any of the hotel's windows.

Placer Town—and Matt Forman—was waiting for him.

Longarm took out his Colt, rested it on his thigh, and kept on riding, a lightning rod waiting for the first quick flash. It came, as he had expected, without warning.

As he passed the black mouth of an alley, the door from the doc's office on the second floor opened. Light flooded the landing as Teresa flung herself out onto it, her hair wild.

"Watch out, Custis!" she cried. "It's a trap!"

A man appeared beside her and clubbed her so hard she toppled down the stairs. He heard the sickening thud as her head struck a step near the bottom. Leaping from his horse, he dashed over to the steps, his .44 out and blazing up at the fellow on the landing, who snapped off two quick shots before ducking back into the doctor's office.

That was the signal.

From the darkened storefronts and windows behind Longarm a barrage opened up. He realized too late he had underestimated the manpower at Matt's disposal. Here was where the Lazy M riders had gone to lick their wounds, and they had been waiting for Matt to arrive. Longarm had obligingly stuck his own head into the trap he had prepared for Matt Forman.

Snatching the unconscious Teresa off the steps, he ducked behind them and did his best to return the fire, doing so judiciously, without panic, aiming at gun flashes and occasionally causing a storefront's window to shiver into a thousand pieces. The stairway made a pretty good barrier to the lead hurled at him, and when the fusillade slackened, Longarm took the chance to reload.

Crouching over Teresa, he heard her groan. He glanced down and saw her eyes flicker as she looked up at him.

"You all right?" he asked.

"I don't think anything's broken, but my head aches."

"No reason it shouldn't, from what I saw."

"I'll be all right."

"Who's upstairs in the doc's office?"

"Two of Matt Forman's riders."

"What're they doing up there?"

"When Matt heard you riding in, he sent them up there to finish off Seth Barton, but Seth and the doc barricaded themselves in the other room."

"And left you behind?"

"They didn't have any choice."

A rifle shot came from the darkened saloon across the street, the bullet biting out a chunk of the stairwell. Both ducked. It was clear new tactics were in order. Matt's men were going to save lead and aim carefully from now on. Longarm pressed Teresa closer to the ground.

"What are you going to do?" she asked. Though her voice was steady, he could feel her shoulders trembling.

"From what you just told me, those two gunslicks in the doc's office are caught between Seth and me. I'm going up there. Keep your head down."

"Be careful."

"I will. And thanks for that warning."

"Remember. I still want to go to Denver."

"And so do I."

One of Forman's riders appeared suddenly from around the corner of the building, a Colt in each hand. Longarm fired at him through the steps and sent a slug crashing into his chest. As the man collapsed facedown in the alley, his fingers squeezed convulsively on the triggers, sending a futile barrage of hot lead into the ground.

Longarm used the commotion to cover him as he ducked around in front of the stairway and charged up the steps. Without pause he kicked open the wooden door. In the light cast by a lamp on the file cabinet, Longarm could see the two gunslicks crouching behind the desk. He flung himself to the floor and shot under the desk, his double-action .44 pumping repeatedly, the slugs tearing into one of the men.

The other one—the same man who had clubbed Teresa—jumped up onto the desk and sent a round down at Longarm. The slug buried itself in the floorboard beside Longarm's cheek. The door behind the desk opened and Seth Barton limped out and swung his crutch at the man, catching him on the back of the neck. There was an ugly crunch. His neck broken, the man toppled off the desk, landing heavily on the floor beside Longarm.

Doc Wolfson, his eyes wild, his face flushed almost crimson, plunged out of the room after Seth, an enormous Remington revolver in his hand.

"Relax, Doc," Longarm told him, getting to his feet.

"What the hell's going on?" Seth demanded. "Teresa was just in here, warning me to get out of town when these two broke in on us."

"It's Matt Forman," Longarm told him, blowing out the lamp. "He's in town with his gunslicks. How's that hip of yours?"

"Still hurts some, but at least I ain't bedridden."

"My God," said Doc Wolfson, peering out the window at the street below. "Here they come! Looks like a small army!"

Longarm stepped to the window. At this height, the moon's pale glow gave him a clear view of Matt's men flitting from storefront to storefront as they closed in, hardware gleaming dully in their fists. And from this side of the street, six more were coming at them. The doc was right: It did look like a small army.

Matt Forman stepped out of the saloon across the street. He had a double-barreled shotgun in his hand. Maybe it was the same one Kate Summerfield had used to scare off Matt's riders that first night. Longarm flung up the window.

"I got you covered, Forman!" he called down to him.

"Goddammit, Long," the man cried, a grudging respect in his voice. "That *was* you on my tail!"

"That's right," Longarm told him. "You should be more careful, Forman."

"You're a lucky man. But your luck has run out now, you son of a bitch."

Forman flung up his shotgun. Before he could fire, Longarm snapped a shot down at him. The bullet shivered the window beside him. He ducked back hastily through the bat-wings without firing.

His men, however, were not as intimidated, and at once sent a wild but steady fusillade through the open window. The upper portion of the window pane disintegrated. Tiny, treacherous glass shards ricocheted about the room like shrapnel. At the same time Longarm could hear the windows in the next room dissolving as they too were taken out.

The three dropped to their hands and knees, listening to the bullets tearing into the ceiling and the walls. Plaster sifted down over them and a few bullets made a wild racket as they slammed into the side of the metal file cabinet. Crouched beside Longarm on the floor, the doc winced as his framed diploma caught two bullets before crashing to the floor. A second later, a ricocheting round disintegrated a bottle of whiskey that had been sitting on a bookshelf.

"My God," Wolfson moaned. "We're none of us goin' to get out of this. Those are wild men down there."

Longarm patted the distraught man on the shoulder and told him to keep his head low. Then he scuttled swiftly across the floor and slipped out onto the landing. Glancing down, he was pleased to see that Teresa had fled from the spot where he had left her.

Lying prone on the landing, he kept his eyes on the alley's entrance, and waited. The rattle of pistol and rifle fire from the street kept steady for a while, then slackened. From the saloon came Matt Forman's voice, issuing curt orders. Longarm heard the dim mutter of discord. There were men who did not want to carry out Matt Forman's bidding.

"Never mind that!" Longarm heard Matt cry harshly, the shrill fury in his voice enough to carry his words across the street. "There ain't a one left up there who ain't hurt! Get up them steps! Finish them off!"

Longarm was suddenly aware of Seth, keeping flat like him, moving out onto the landing to join him. Seth was carrying the doc's huge Remington.

"Let the bastards come," Seth muttered. "It's about time I paid them back for this bum hip."

"Wait'll I say to fire."

Seth nodded.

Then came the sound of hurrying feet and the chink of spurs as Forman's men approached the alley entrance. There was a momentary pause, some hurried whispering, then, out of the darkness and the alley, Forman's gunslicks poured. Without pause they swarmed up the steps. It was a damn fool rush into hellfire and brimstone for those leading the charge. But then, Longarm realized, these men would not be in Matt Forman's employ if they had any sense to begin with.

Longarm held his fire until the first two men were close enough for him to reach out and touch.

"Now!" Longarm cried.

He squeezed his trigger and felt the Colt pulse and jump in his hand like something alive. Beside him, Seth's big Remington hammered away, its blast almost deafening Longarm. He saw the hail storm of lead kicking up dust on the men's vests and jackets as the terrible, withering fire sent the men in front hurtling backward upon the heads and shoulders of those behind them.

The carnage was sickening. The cries and screams of wounded men filled the night. Those hit by the men toppling backward struck the ground at the foot of the stairs, and were then buried by the wounded men tumbling onto them. Only one man prevented himself from falling back down the steps. He had ducked low and clung to the bannister. Straightening up less than five steps away, he saw Longarm's muzzle yawning down at him.

Longarm held his fire.

"Get out of here, mister!" he growled.

Slapping his Colt back into his holster, the gunslick spun about and plunged down the steps. Leaping over the tangled, groaning men at the bottom, he vanished

172

around the corner. A moment later Longarm heard the sound of a galloping horse, its staccato beat fading rapidly. Those at the foot of the stairway able to stand pulled free of the wounded men. When one of them was foolish enough to raise his gun to fire at Longarm, Seth stopped him with a single bullet to the head.

That ended the revolution.

Those that could raced back out of the alley and scattered. Longarm jumped up and raced down the stairs and across the street, shouldering through the bat-wings of The Owl Hoot saloon. The inside of the place was pitch-black. He did not stand exposed in the doorway, but dove to the floor behind the bar just as Matt Forman, barricaded behind an overturned table, fired at him. The buckshot shattered the mirror and exploded the neat pyramids of glasses on the shelves in front of it, sending a shower of broken glass rattling down onto Longarm's hat brim.

Longarm could hear Matt slipping two more shells into his shotgun, then snapping it shut. The safety clicked off and Matt yelled, "Stick your head up, asshole, and I'll blow it off for you. I missed with a sixgun, but I won't with this!"

Longarm poked his head up, snapped a shot at Forman, and heard the slug rip harmlessly into the table. Forman's shotgun roared back at him. The upper portion of the bar absorbed the buckshot, and a few more splinters from the mirror showered down on Longarm. He swore softly as he heard Forman's deep chuckle. This was a standoff and Forman knew it.

The cold muzzle of a revolver came to rest on the back of his neck. He froze. Kate's voice came soft and clear to him. She had moved down the bar in the darkness and was crouched beside him.

"I want you to let him go, Custis."

"Ride out, you mean?"

"Yes."

"I can't do that."

"Why not? You got Gil. You got the man you came for."

"Gil didn't kill the girl, Matt did."

"Matt?"

"Gil was covering for Matt. That's the truth of it, Kate."

Forman could hear them talking and recognized Kate's voice. "Kate, that you over there?" he called.

"Yes, it's me, Matt."

"You want to get your head blown off? Get out of here!"

"I'm saving your hide, Matt."

"Damn it, Kate. I got this son of a bitch dead to rights. Soon as he shows his head, I'll blow it off."

"The only thing you're blowing up is my saloon. I got him covered, Matt. Get out of town and take your gunslicks with you."

Longarm heard Matt get to his feet, chuckling. "Sure thing, Kate. Anything you say—soon as I finish off this bastard. Just keep him covered and I'll take him off your hands."

"You come over here and I'll shoot you."

"I don't believe you, Kate. That son of a bitch killed Gil and Clem Jagger!"

"And I suppose at the time both men were just standing around picking their noses."

"Damn it, Kate. That's my brother Gil you're talkin' about!"

"I don't care, Matt. His death is on your hands, not this fellow Long."

"You mean you're standing up for a lawman?"

"Move out, Matt. I'll have no killin' in my saloon."

"This ain't fair, Kate."

"What's fair, Matt? Killin' that girl in Denver? Shooting up this town? Sending two of your thugs over there to kill Seth Barton?"

Longarm heard Matt fling down his shotgun, then heard the tramp of his boots. As Matt neared the bat-wings, Kate increased the pressure of her revolver on the back of Longarm's neck. Before Matt stepped out of the saloon, he paused to look back at Longarm and Kate standing up now in the darkness behind the bar.

"You'll regret this, Kate!"

"Get out, Matt. Now. While you still can ride."

With a bitter curse, Matt strode from the saloon.

Longarm felt Kate move away from him. When he heard her place the revolver down on top of the bar, he pushed out past her and hurried to the bat-wings.

"Custis," she called after him urgently. "Let him go. He's not worth it. I know that now."

Reaching the bat-wings, Longarm peered out. Kate hurried from behind the bar and stood beside him. Matt Forman was astride his horse, calling to those of his men who still could ride to mount up. Longarm could see Seth Barton in the alley across the street, gun in hand, flat against the side of the building as he watched Forman warily. The doc was dimly visible in the alley tending to those wounded who still could benefit from his care.

For a reason Longarm could not understand, the rage that had governed him for so long drained away. He decided he would leave Matt Forman to whatever furies he had yet to encounter.

"Go on, Forman," Longarm snapped, striding out onto the porch. "Ride out. Now. While you still can."

Without argument, Matt and three other riders, one of them sagging loosely over the pommel of his saddle, rode past the saloon, heading out of town. They had almost vanished into the night when Longarm heard shouts and a flurry of gunfire, followed by the sudden clatter of hooves. Striding off the saloon porch, Longarm looked up the street and saw a whirlwind of spinning horsemen, gun flashes lighting their faces.

Above the shouts and cries he recognized Tenny's voice, cursing with a resonant fury. Then out of the melee burst Matt Forman on foot, a hard-riding horseman chasing him. The rider cut the fleeing man down with a single round, then pulled up beside him to punch shot after shot into his writhing figure.

"Matt! Oh, my God," breathed Kate, as she hurried down the porch steps and ran up the street.

Longarm kept pace with her, pulling up alongside the still-mounted Tenny as Kate flung herself to the ground beside Matt. Forman's chest was dark with blood, his face slack. Kate cradled his head in her lap, crooning softly to him. Longarm could not fathom her grief. Matt Forman was a reptile, and Kate knew this as well as anyone. Once more the vagaries of the female mind eluded Longarm, as they would forever.

Two of the men who had been riding out with Forman had broken free and were gone, the sound of their pounding hooves faded rapidly. The wounded rider, however, lay facedown on the ground, as still as death. As Doc Wolfson ran up to tend to him, Tenny dismounted. The rest of his weary riders, about six of them, did the same.

"You're a sight for sore eyes, Long," Tenny said, grinning. "Tom Goodnight said you were dead."

Ellen Buckman and Teresa appeared out of the darkness. "Did I hear you mention Tom?" Ellen asked Tenny urgently. "Did he ride back with you?"

"'Fraid he didn't, Ellen."

"Where is he?"

"I left him in Silver Creek."

"I don't understand."

Tenny looked at Longarm, unwilling to address Ellen directly. "Silver Creek will be a smoking ruin until the first snow hits it, Long. You might say I finished what you started. I don't expect any more buyers'll be using that place to contract for stolen beef."

"Tenny," Ellen persisted. "What do you mean, you left Tom in Silver Creek? Has he been hurt?"

Giving up on his effort to shield Ellen, Tenny turned to face her. "What I'm sayin', Ellen, is that Tom was in this with Matt Forman. All the way. And when he and Forman's gunslicks tried to defend some beef we'd liberated from the burnout, there was a firefight. He got shot up bad."

Ellen's face went paper-white. "How bad?"

177

"He's dead, Ellen."

Ellen gasped. "I don't believe you! Tom would not work with Matt Forman. He hated the man! You killed him for no reason!"

"No, Ellen," Longarm told her patiently, stepping closer. "It won't do to blame Tenny. Tom sat his horse beside Matt. The two of them plotted to take over the whole range. I was flat on my back at the time and couldn't move. They both assumed I was dead."

Her hand over her mouth, Ellen looked from Longarm to Tenny, disbelief giving way now to horror. She was realizing in that moment the full extent of Tom Goodnight's betrayal—of her as well as of her dead father.

Longarm thought she was going to faint. Teresa stepped between them and put her arms about Ellen to support her. Kate had overheard everything. Leaving Matt Forman's side, she took Ellen about the shoulder and guided her off in the direction of her house, leaving Teresa behind.

Sheriff Blount and the town constable appeared, like rats chased out of a town dump. They looked uncomfortably down at Matt Forman's sprawled body, then up at Tenny and his ring of weary, glowering riders. In a voice laced with contempt, Tenny told them they were not needed, then ordered them to go fetch the undertaker. The two scurried off.

"That's all them buzzards are good for," Tenny remarked, watching them go. "If I have anything to say about it, there'll be some new elections in this town pretty damn soon."

Seth, using his crutch with great dexterity, swung out

178

of the darkness and pulled up beside Longarm. "I just saw Ellen. She was crying. What happened, Long?"

"Tom Goodnight's dead. He was in all this with Matt Forman."

Seth swore softly.

"You know Ellen?"

"She's been very . . . kind these past days while I was getting used to the crutches."

"Maybe you better go see her then. She could use a kind word. Tell her for me that, despite everything, I'm sorry about Tom."

"Think maybe I'll do that," Seth replied.

As Seth swung off, Wolfson hurried over to kneel beside Matt Forman's sprawled body. His inspection did not last long. Dropping his stethoscope back into his black bag, he stood up, smiling with considerable relief at Longarm.

"Matt Forman's gone. Now maybe this town can go back to sleep."

Longarm did not reply as he looked around him at the dim faces peering at them from both sidewalks. As soon as the shooting had stopped, the townspeople had appeared out of the night like cats, a great silent watchful crowd drawn by the smell of death. At the sight of their dark ranks, Longarm realized that all he wanted now was to leave these hills and put this grim, death-ridden town behind him.

He felt Teresa step closer to him, then gently rest her hand on his arm. He turned and looked down at her face, her smile causing it to bloom like a dark flower in the night.

"Will you take me from here now?" she asked softly.

He squeezed her hand. "First thing in the morning."

"Denver?"

"Yes."

"Are you all right?"

"There's a . . . weariness."

"I will comfort you. Come."

He bid good-bye to Tenny and the doc, and with Teresa at his side, pushed his way through the crowd.

Chapter 11

Longarm poured Marshal Billy Vail another drink. The chief had greeted him warmly, his round, well-fed face creased in a grin. It was obvious Vail was glad to have him back on fully legal duty once more.

The whiskey was the best Maryland rye stocked by the Windsor, and that was fine with Longarm. He was celebrating. It was late in the afternoon. Teresa and he had finished a shopping trip, and she was waiting for him now up in her room. Billy Vail had just got back from a trip to Washington, and had stopped by to hear Longarm's report on Aleta Crowley's killer. Longarm had just given it to him.

Billy Vail threw down the rye, coughing silently as the hot liquor scalded his tonsils. "And you're certain it was Matt Forman, not his brother, who killed the Crowley girl."

"Yes."

"I'll make it a point to see Jim Crowley before Monday."

"You only need to tell him that Aleta's killer is dead."

"You don't have to remind me of that, Custis. Besides, I don't have to believe everything Gil Forman told you, not if I don't want to."

Longarm nodded without comment, and for a while the two men nursed their drinks in silence. Longarm had known Jim Crowley's girl only fleetingly, but Vail had known her since her seventh birthday.

Then Vail spoke up. "You say Seth Barton is okay?"

"He's going to be the next sheriff of Sheridan County, and from what I gather, he's hitting it off pretty well with Ellen Buckman."

"He should do fine."

"Did you hear anything in Washington about the trouble up there?"

Chuckling softly, Vail reached for the bottle and poured himself another snifter. "Now that you mention it, there was a telegram from the governor of Montana Territory. Seems there were reports of a range war brewing in the mountains. They asked what I might know about it. I said I hadn't the slightest idea what was going on, but that I'd ask you about it when you got back from a fishing trip you was taking up there, you and a deputy marshal from Utah."

"Now you can make your report."

"I can. There is no longer any range war in that high country." He smiled. "And you came back, as usual, with a fine catch."

Longarm finished his drink. "She's upstairs now, waiting."

Billy Vail sighed and reached for his hat. "Thanks for the drink. I'll expect you in the office first thing Monday morning."

"I'll think about it. Teresa's all fired anxious for me to take her to see San Francisco."

"I won't let you go, Custis. I need you here."

Vail slapped his hat on and strode out of the hotel saloon. Longarm dropped coins on the table to cover his bill, left the saloon, and mounted the lobby's wide marble stairs to the second floor. A moment later, Teresa pulled the door of her room open, and he stepped inside. Her hair was combed out, and she had put on a light-blue dressing gown, one of the three new gowns she had purchased that day.

"I thought I'd let you see how it looked on me," she told him, closing the door. "Before we go out for dinner."

"It looks fine," he told her, handing her his hat and shrugging out of his coat. "But do we have to go out for dinner?"

She smiled. "I'm way ahead of you. I already called room service."

He started to unbutton his shirt. She saw his intent, walked past him, and hung a Do Not Disturb sign on the outside knob. Then she drew him over to the bed.

"When are we leaving for San Francisco?"

"Billy says he needs me here."

"Drat!"

He put his arms around her and pulled her down beside him on the bed, and felt her agile fingers swiftly,

183

expertly unbuttoning his fly. He peeled down his pants and kicked them off. She helped with the rest and thrust herself close against him, and he realized she was wearing nothing at all under the silken gown.

"We'll go to San Francisco some other time," he told her, easing himself gently into her.

Her thighs lifted and her legs tightened about his waist. He pushed forward and rose up over her, kissing her on her eyelids, her nose, then her lips. Her arms tightened about his neck, her legs still scissoring his waist.

"You know what?" she asked, her eyes shining.

"No. What?"

"I think I'm going to like it here in Denver."

"That's my girl."

A little later, the boy from room service knocked softly to indicate their dinner was outside the door on its cart. Neither of them paid the slightest attention, which meant their dinner would be cold when they got to it.

Not that they would notice.

Watch for

LONGARM AND THE QUIET GUNS

one hundred and fourteenth novel
in the bold LONGARM series from Jove

coming in June!